LuVMachinZ Collection #1

Art of Love

written & illustrated
by Markieji

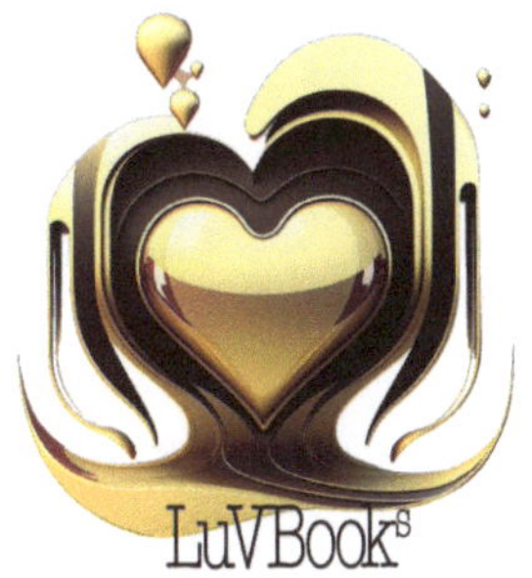

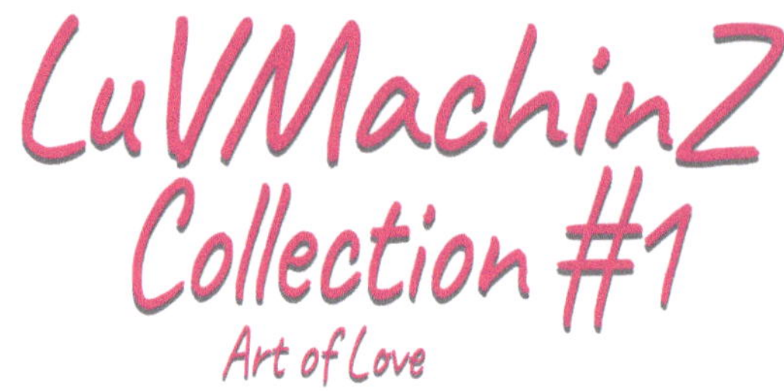

ISBN: 979-8-218-32175-8

to
My Angel

"Love everyone, including yourself."

Baba Hari Har Ramji

LuVMachinZ

There are at least 96 words for love in Sanskrit. Each of these words expresses a distinct aspect or quality of love.

English has only one word that directly translates into love, and that is, of course, "love."

The LuV MachinZ in this collection symbolize love in its many forms and expressions. These iconic forces are all around us. They encourage and create the conditions for kindness, compassion, and romance.

The Power of Love

LuV MachinZ are literally a labor of love that began as designs for Valentine's cards and evolved into a symbolic exploration into the Power of Love.

Symbols are powerfully influential because they connect directly with the core of our beliefs. The images that populate our minds create our world.

With LuV MachinZ my hope is to give a humorous shape and form to interactions with those around us. The Art of Love seeks to open a portal to transcendence and visualize the divinity of love and life.

Grounded in unconditional love, LuV MachinZ express the ability to give love without an expectation of receiving something in return. Therein is the true Power of Love.

Love is the only thing that can be given away without being diminished. The more you give, the more you have to give.

Love that's given freely and without obligation or the expectation of something in exchange, elevates our presence in the world and nurtures our soul.

I hope the LuV MachinZ find a place in your heart and bring the Power of Love to you and those you hold dear.

Markieji

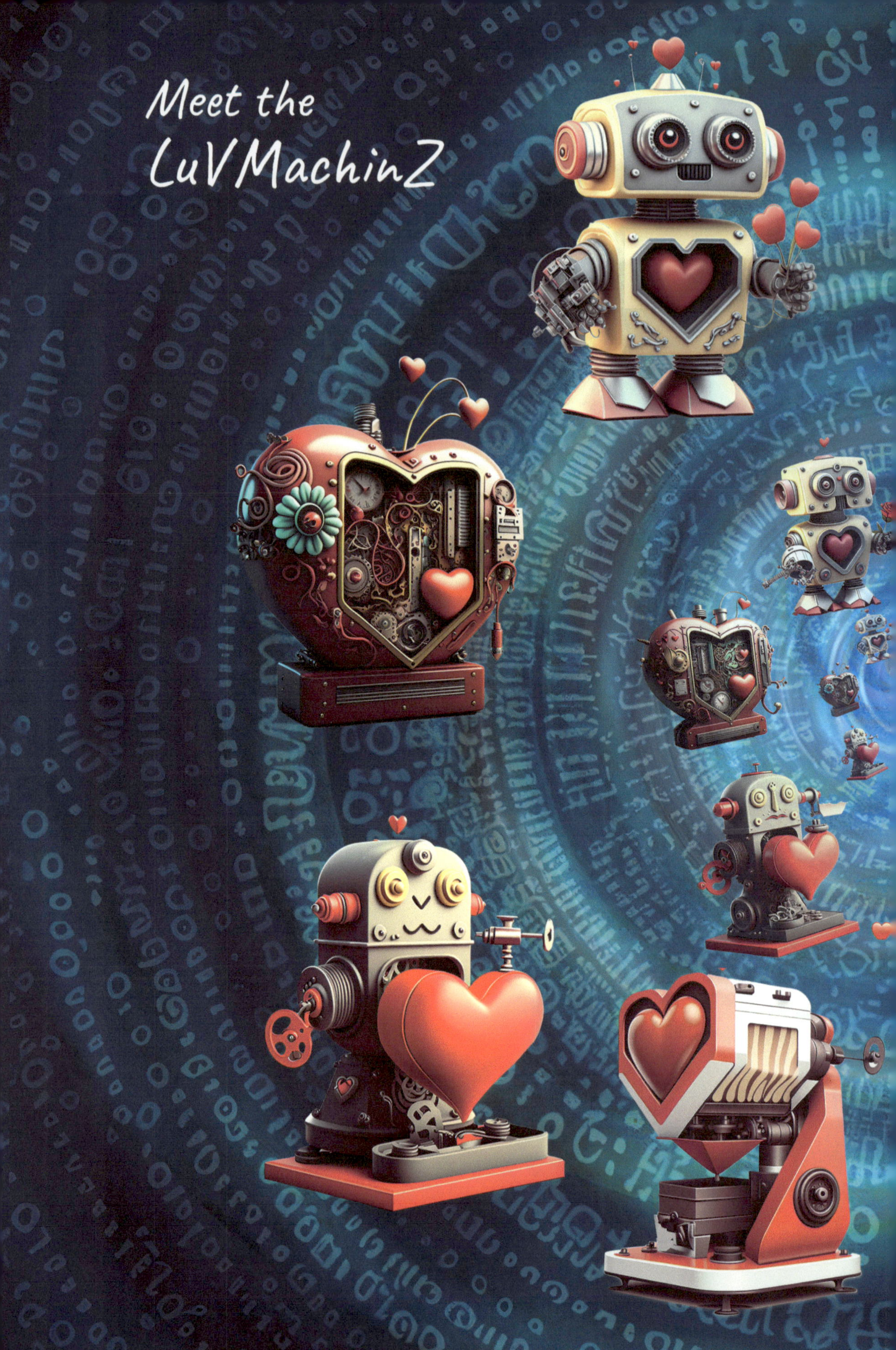
Meet the
LuVMachinZ

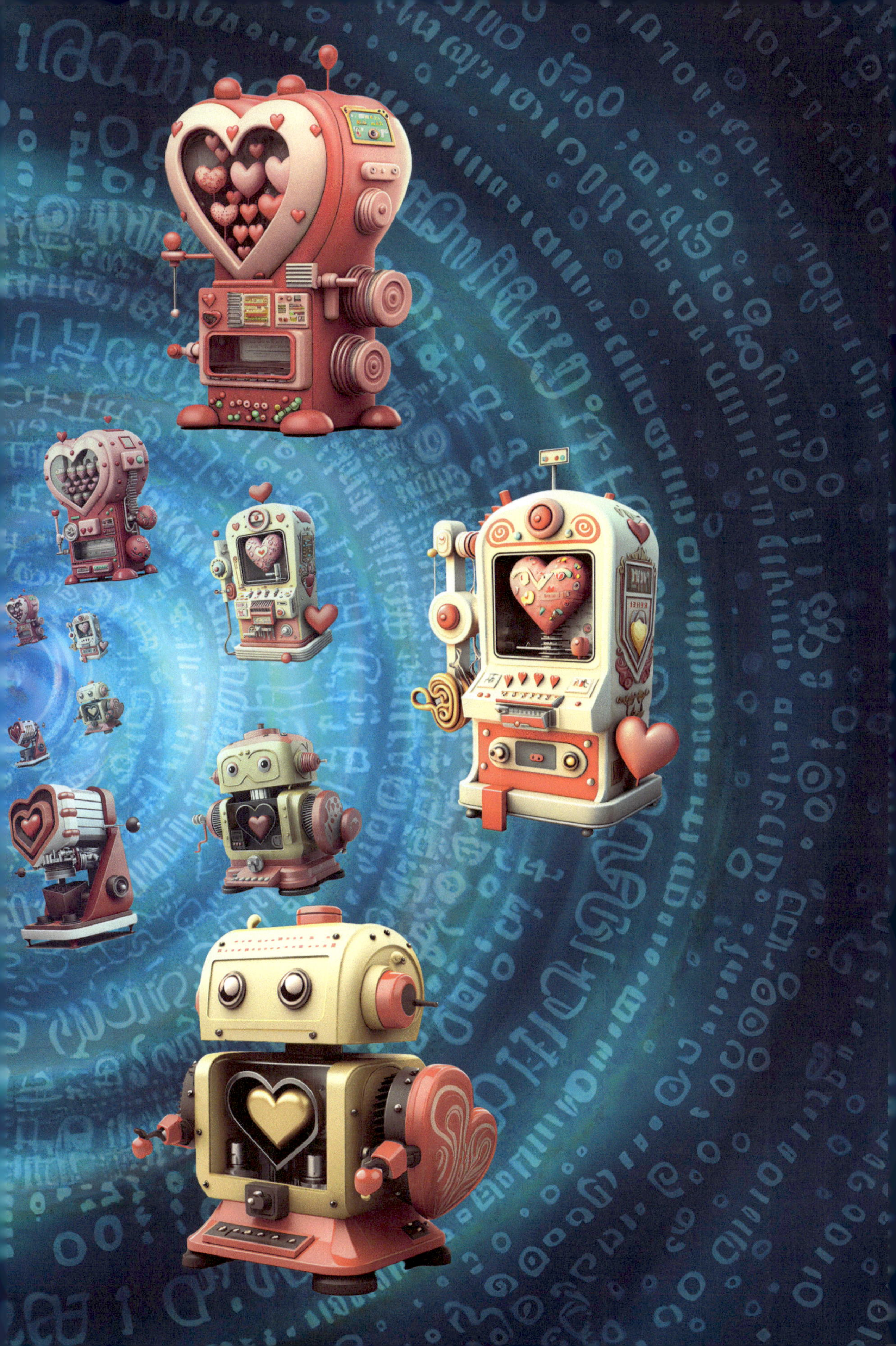

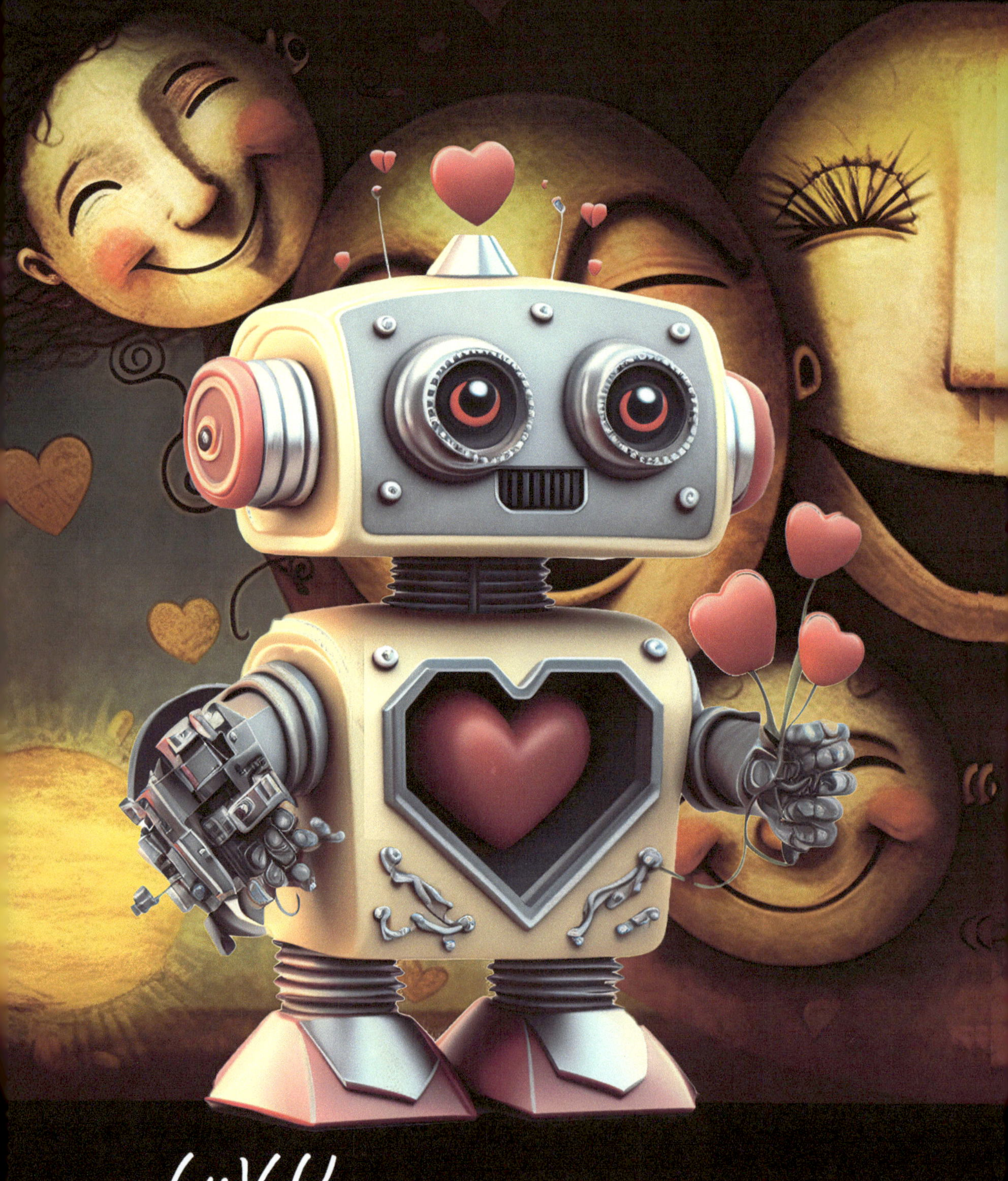
LuVU

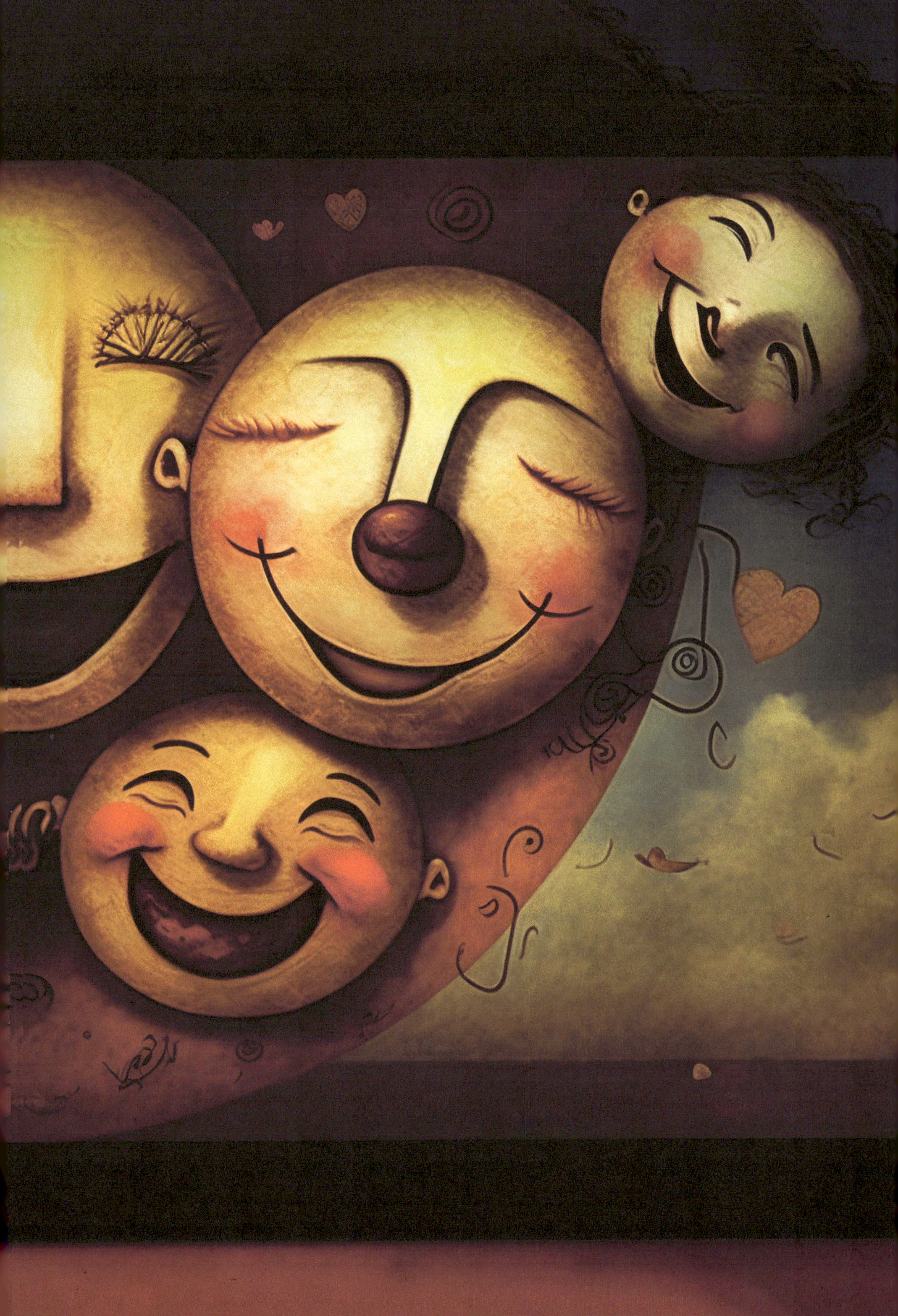

LuV U

LuV U offers gifts of flowers and magical hearts, and opens things that were not made for human hands. LuV U takes on hard plastic containers or packages that are impossible to open. Those items causing "wrap-rage" which takes us far from love.

LuV U keeps us peaceful, calm, and happy - and only wants to make love flow.

Seeing only love, LuV U guides our way and helps us to find love in each and every way.

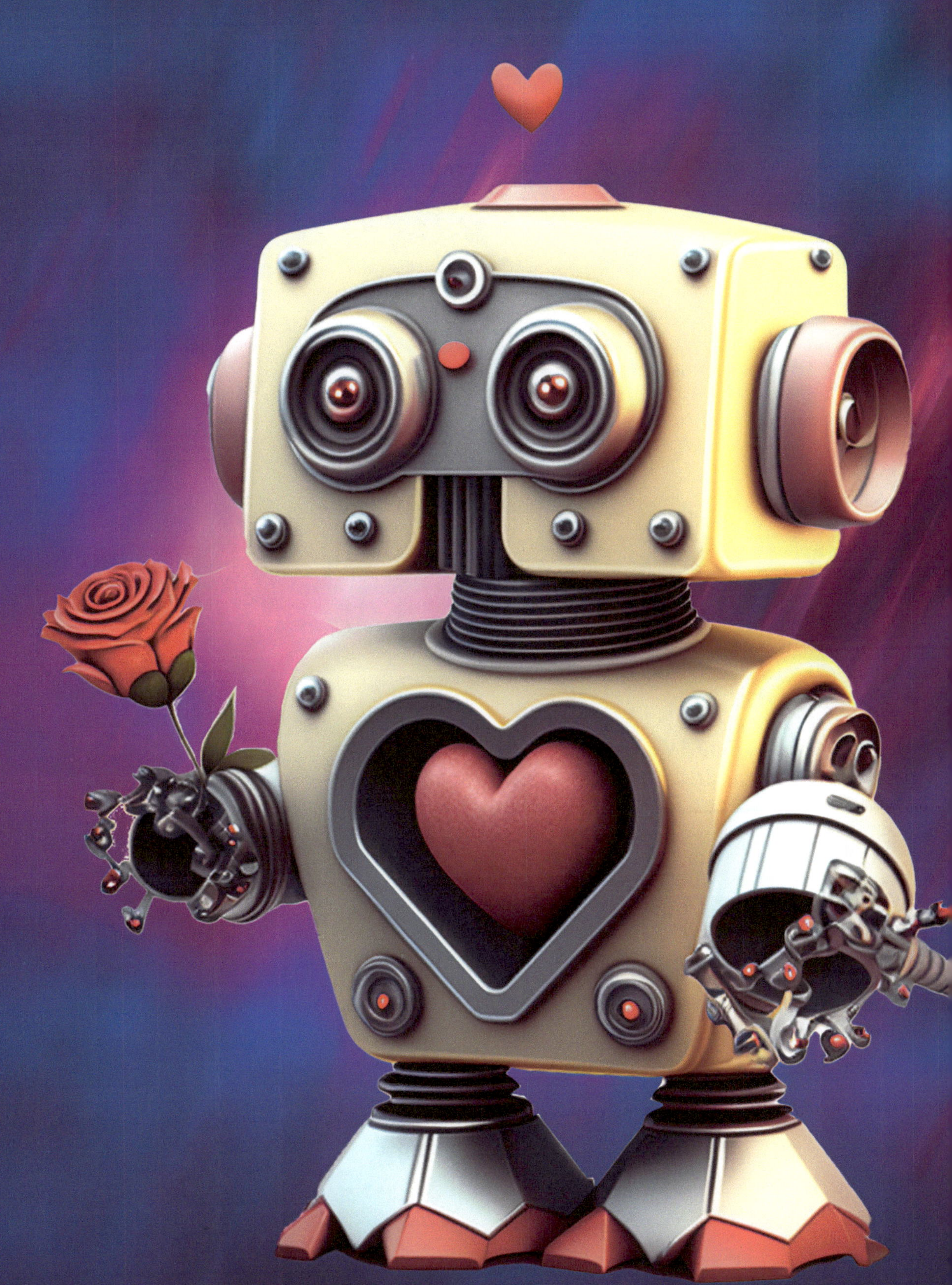

LuV U is caring, compasionate and hopelessly romantic

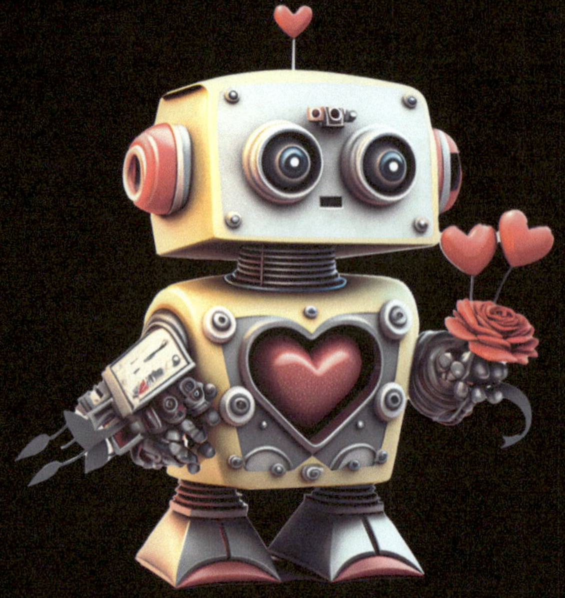

LuV U 1700

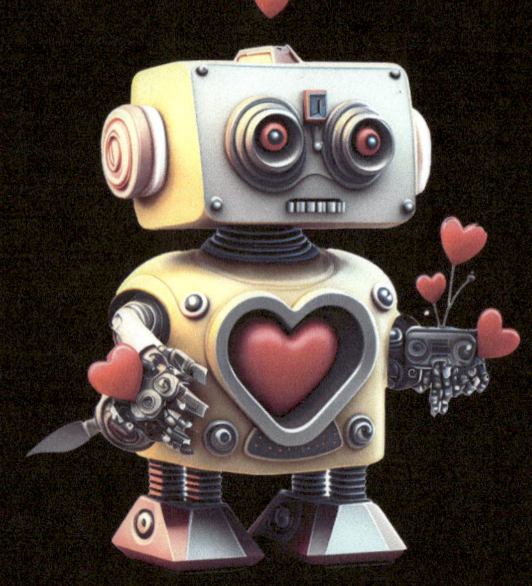

LuV U 1701

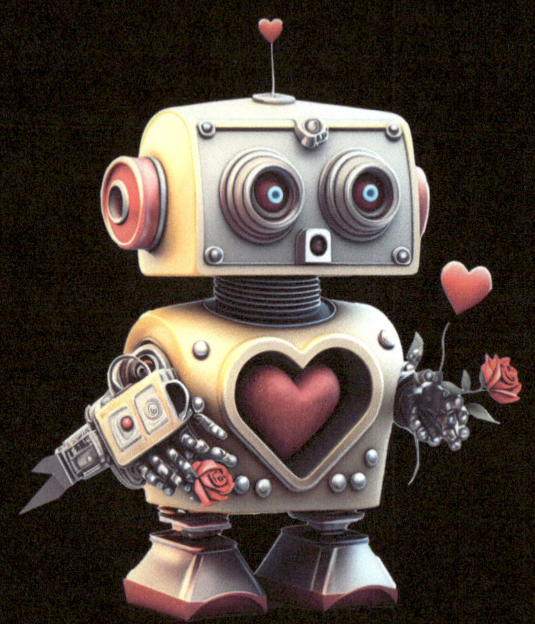

LuV U 1704

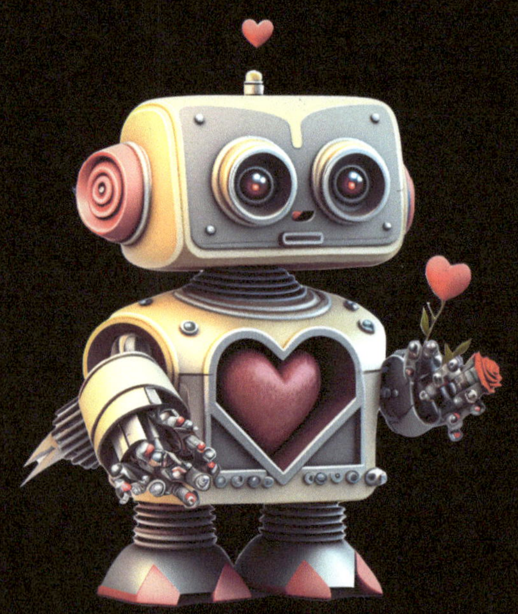

LuV U 1705

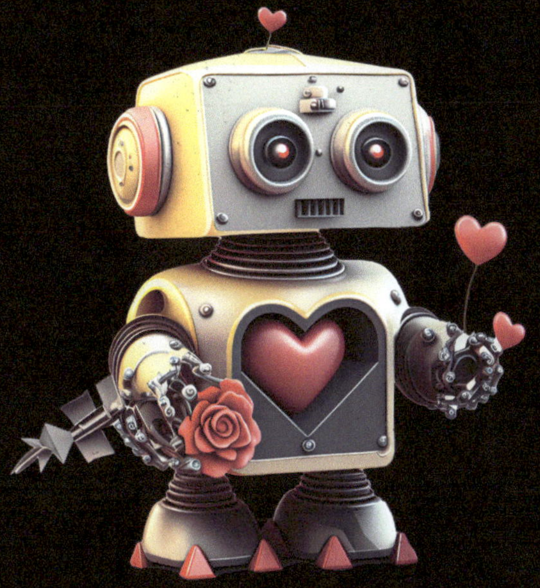

LuV U 1702

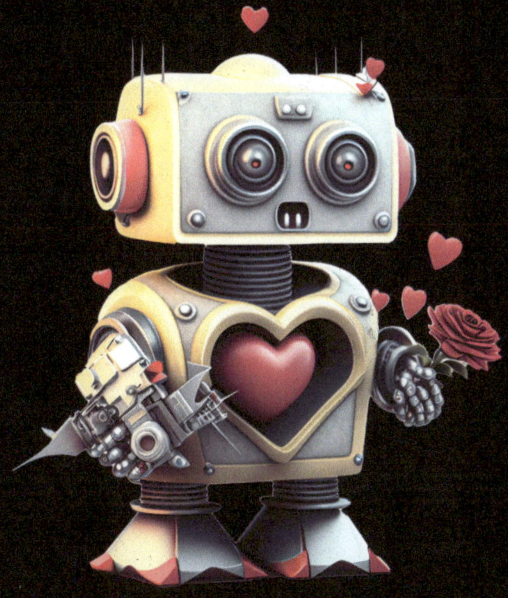

LuV U 1703

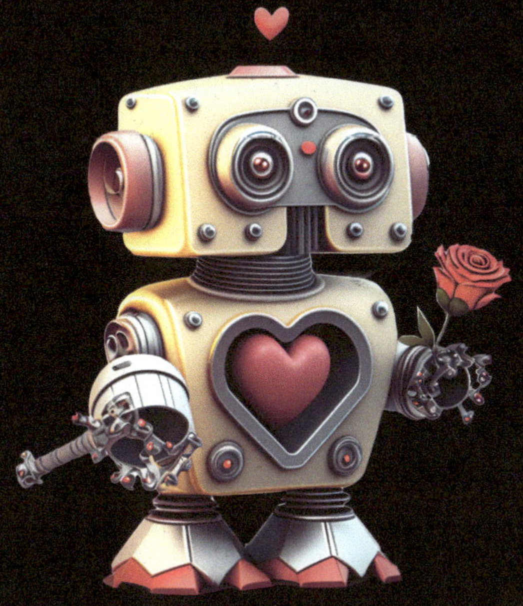

LuV U 1706

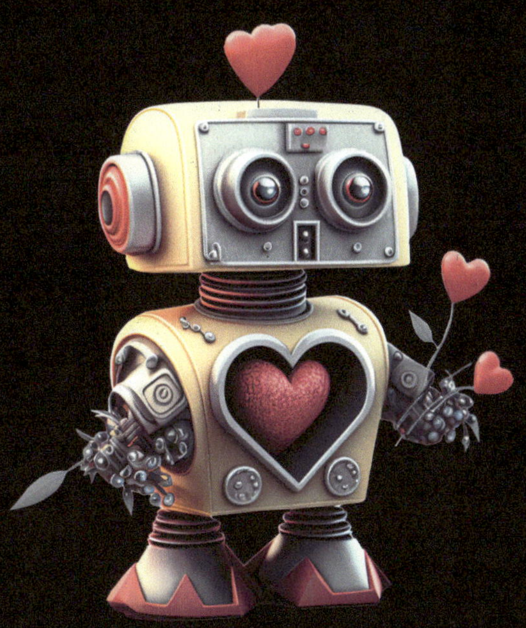

LuV U 1707

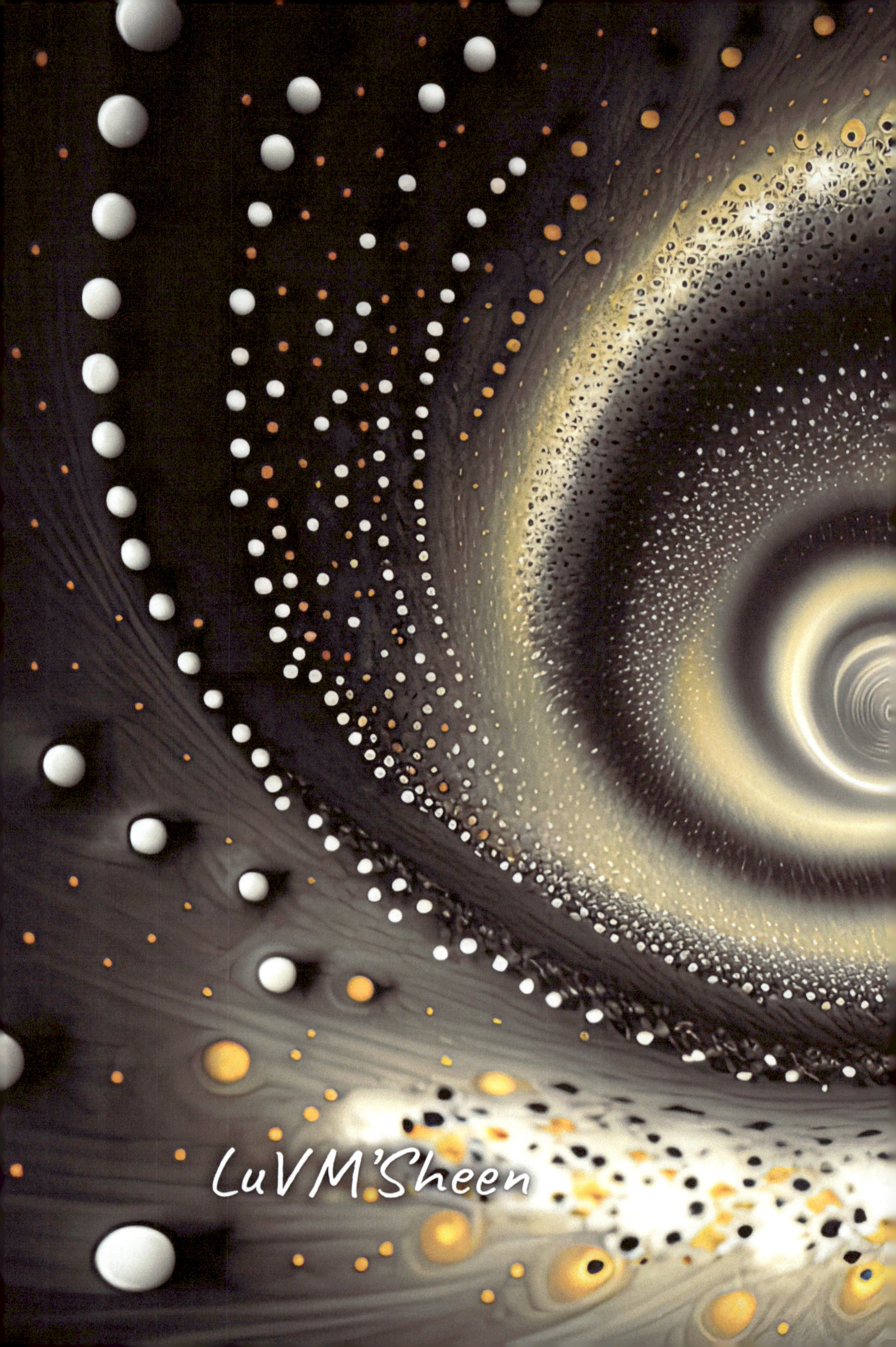
LuVM'Sheen

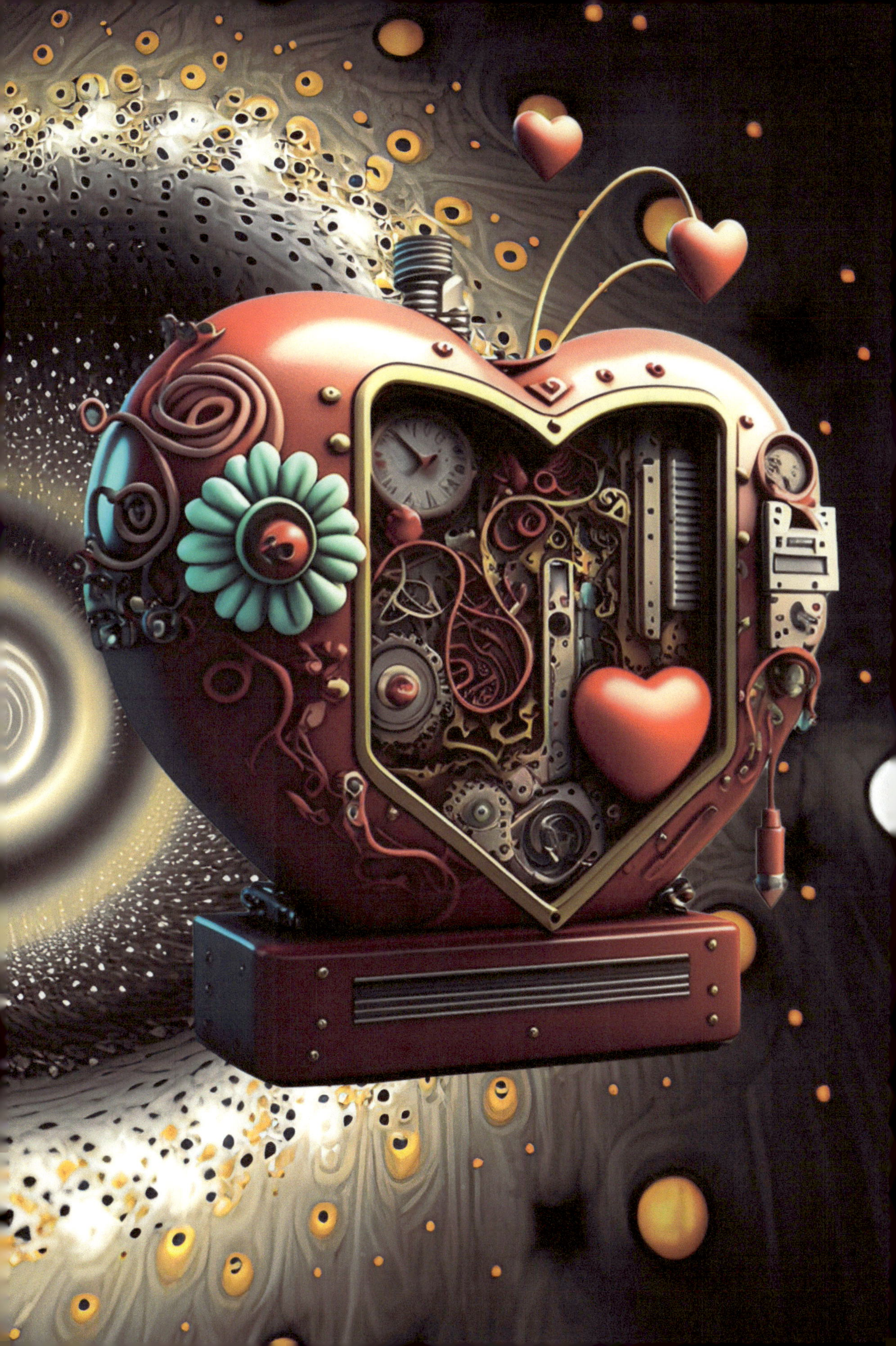

LuV M'Sheen

LuV M' Sheen feels the love that runs through every heart, and everything that has a heart is connected to M' Sheen.

M' Sheen never falters or fades as it gives the gift of love. Its soul flows through each one of us as a witness to desire. It keeps fortune, hope, and dreams alive.

We LOVE M' Sheen for its power and devotion. Its essence is our life.

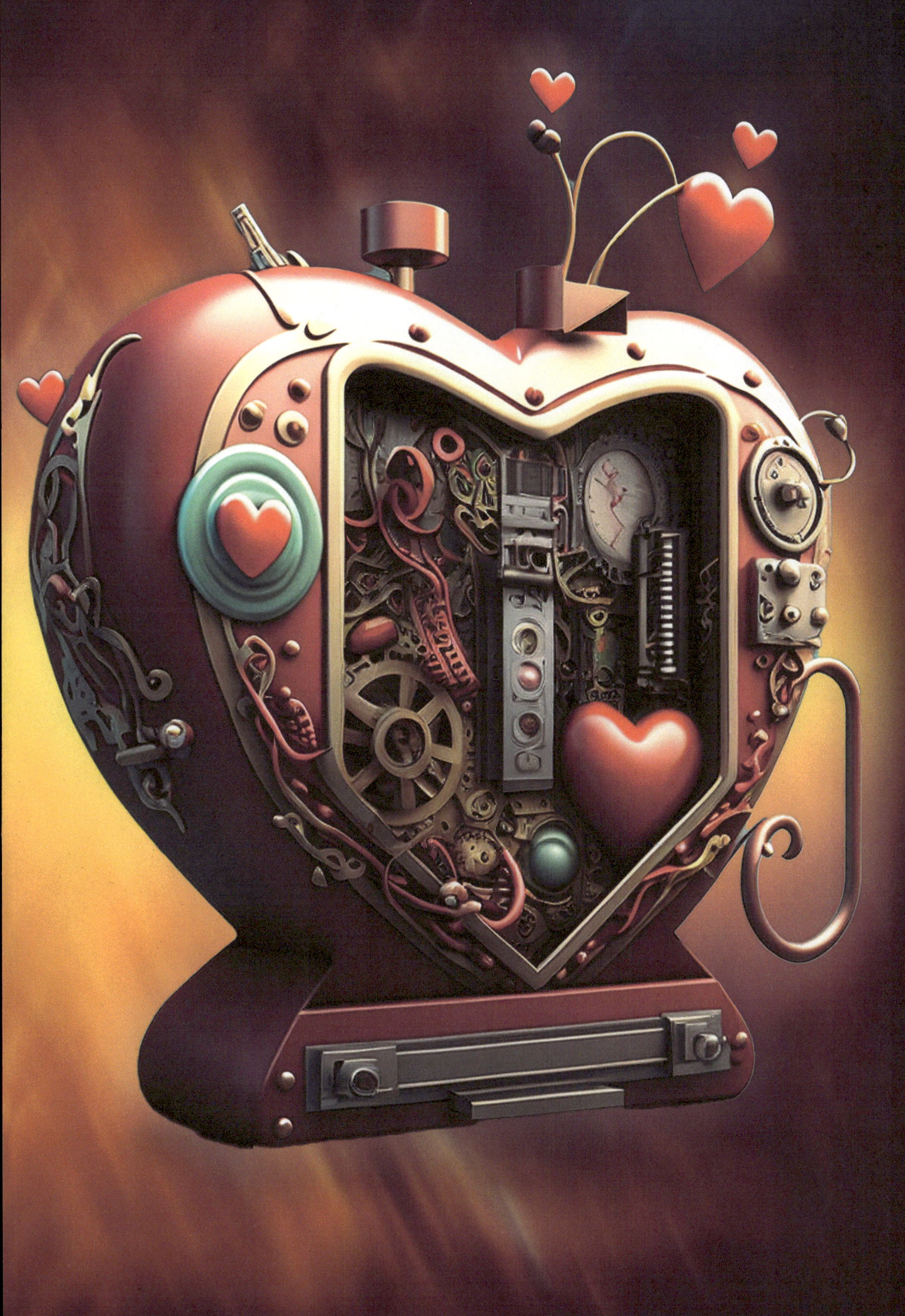

LuV M'Sheen holds the mystery of life itself

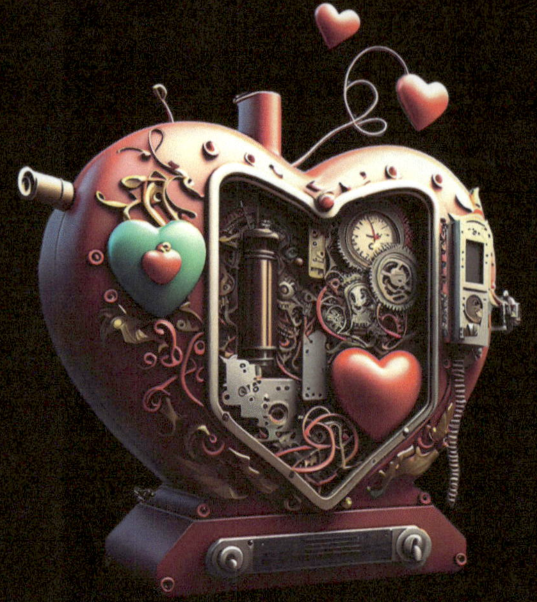

LuV M'Sheen 701

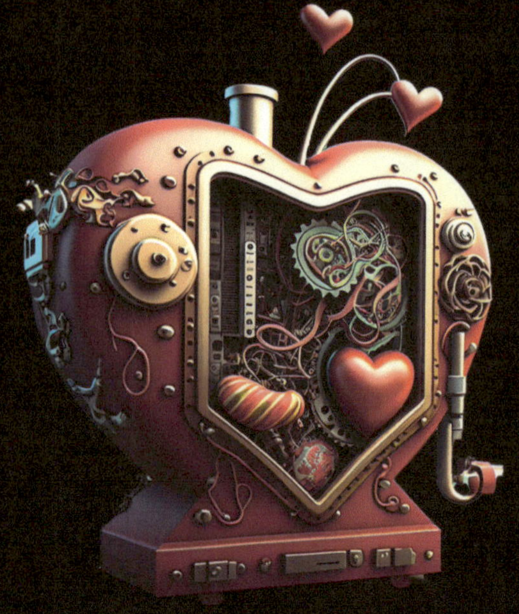

LuV M'Sheen 702

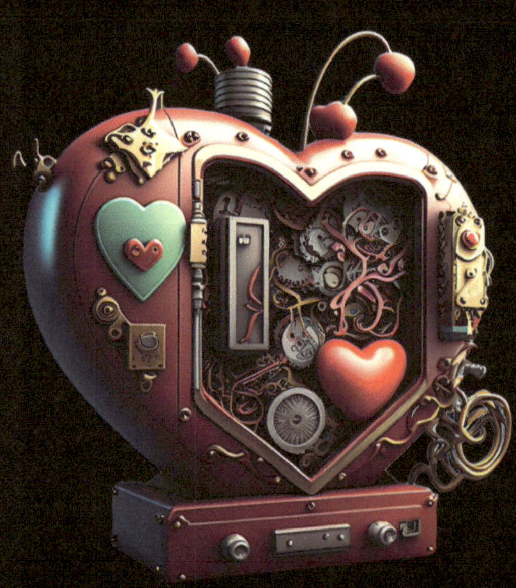

LuV M'Sheen 705

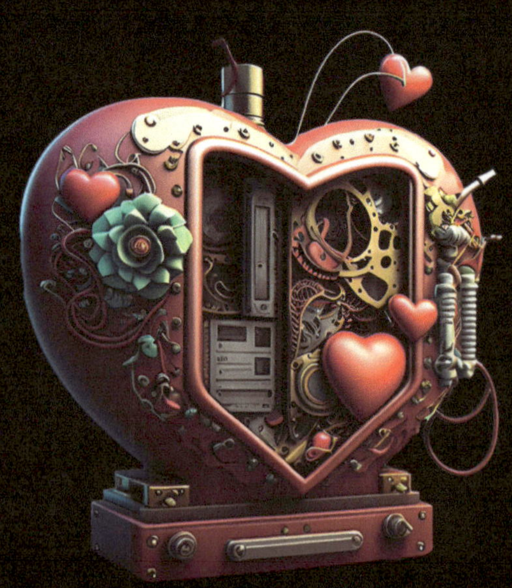

LuV M'Sheen 706

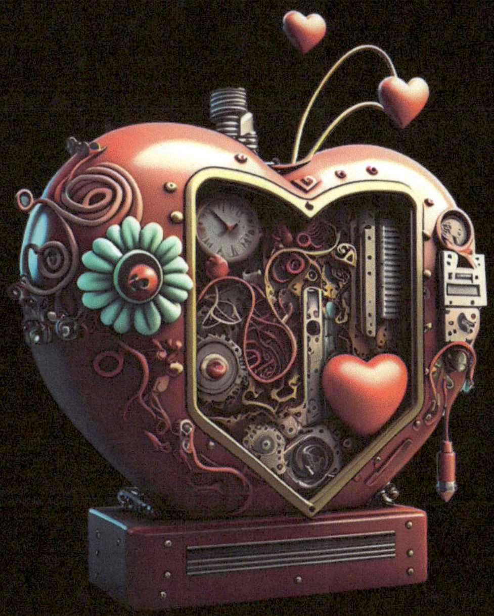

LuV M'Sheen 703

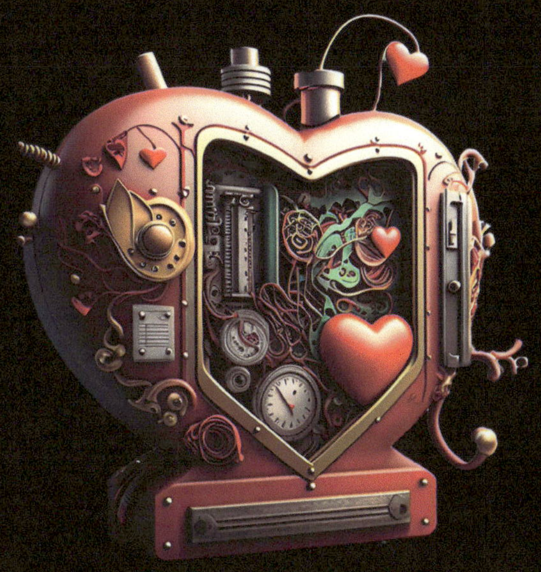

LuV M'Sheen 704

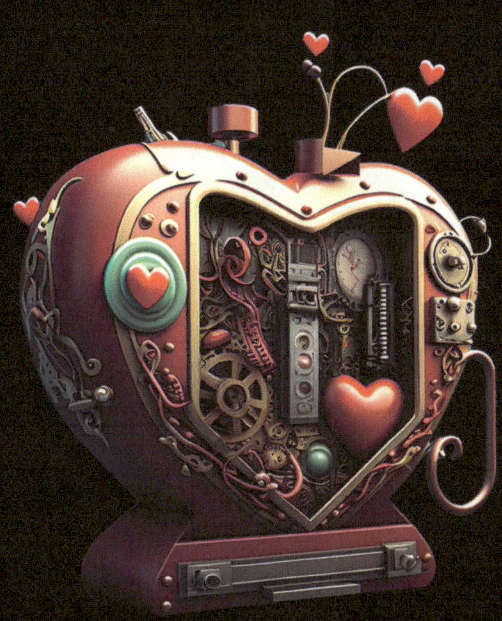

LuV M'Sheen 707

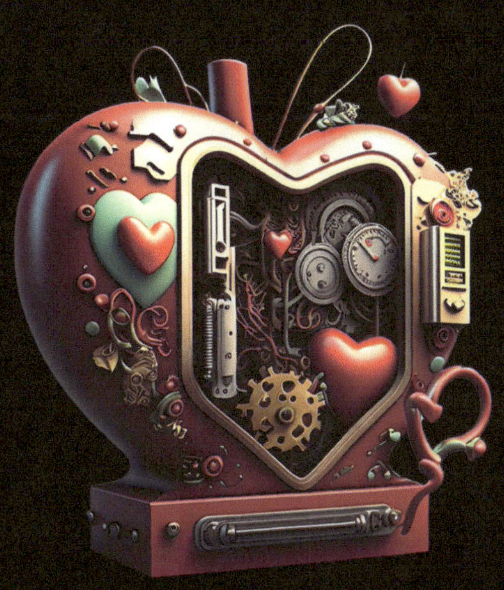

LuV M'Sheen 708

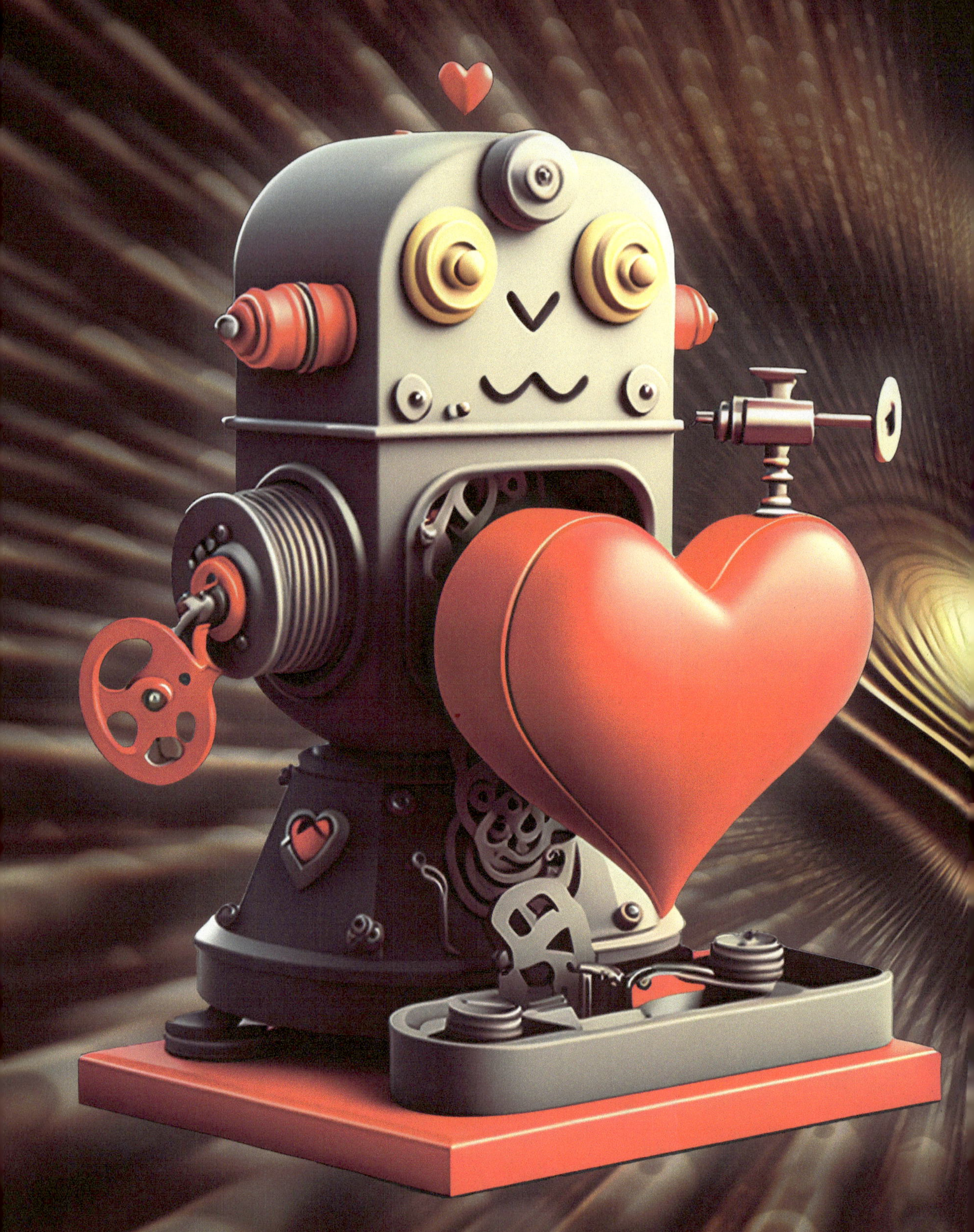

Heart Throb

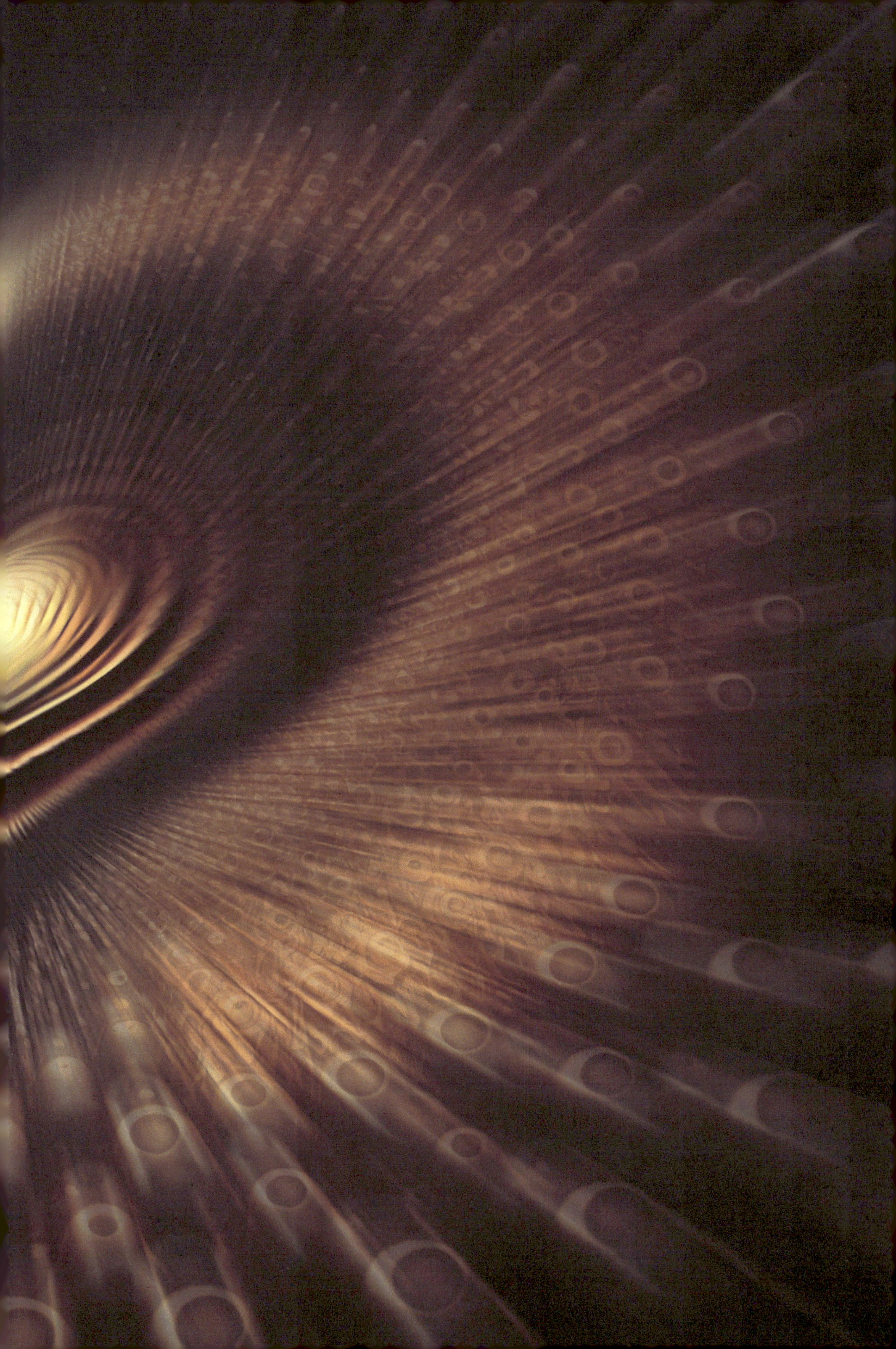

Heart Throb

Heart Throb is the star of every story and the wind in every sail. Its passion is so powerful it is impossible to ignore.

Heart Throb opens hidden doors and lives for new adventures. It dazzles and beguiles us as it urges pure freedom.

When Heart Throb's passion rises, its fire stirs our soul. No force can stop the ardor from which its rapture flows. Embarking on life's journey it calls us once again.

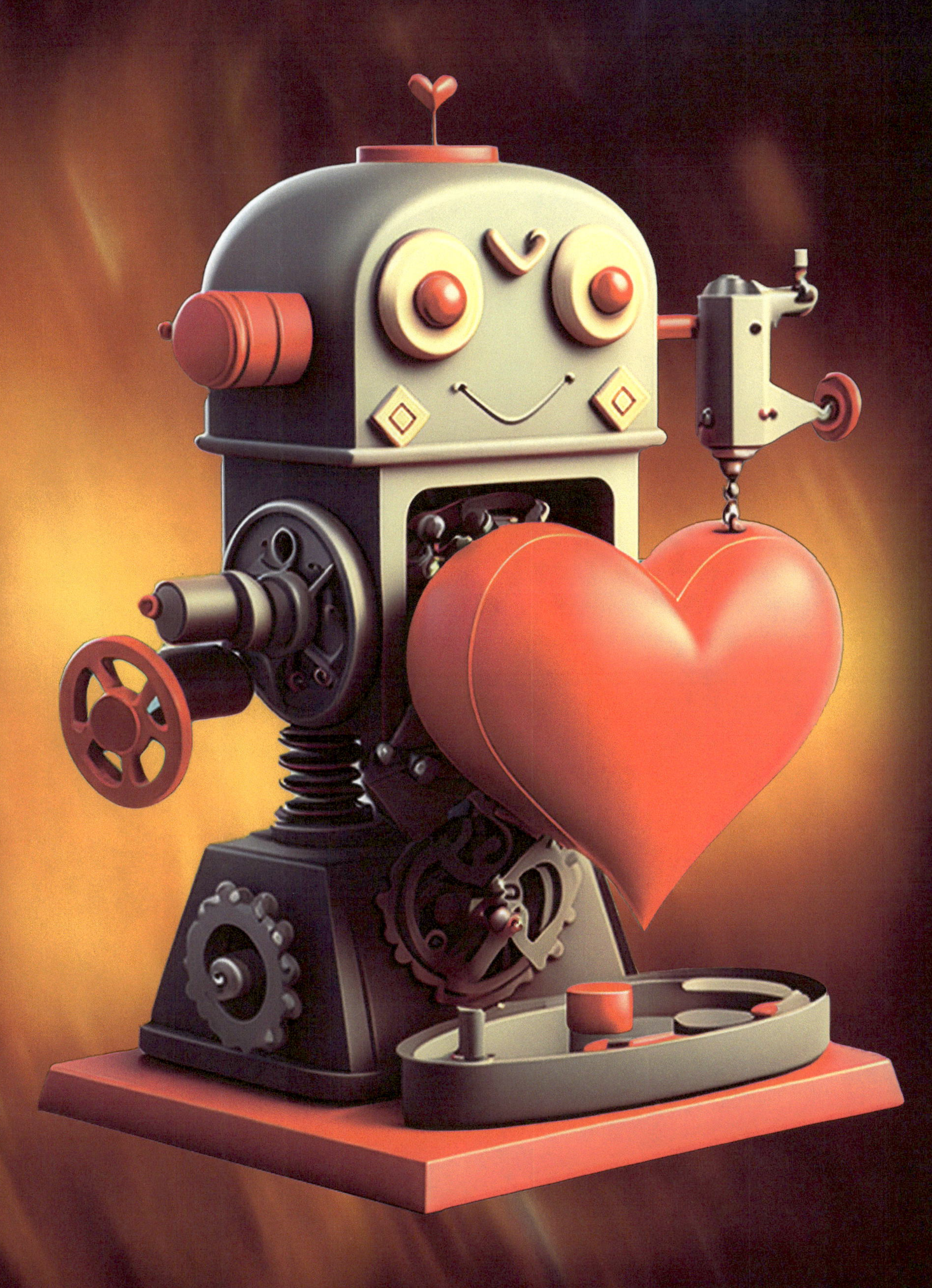

Heart Throb is guided by love and driven by passion

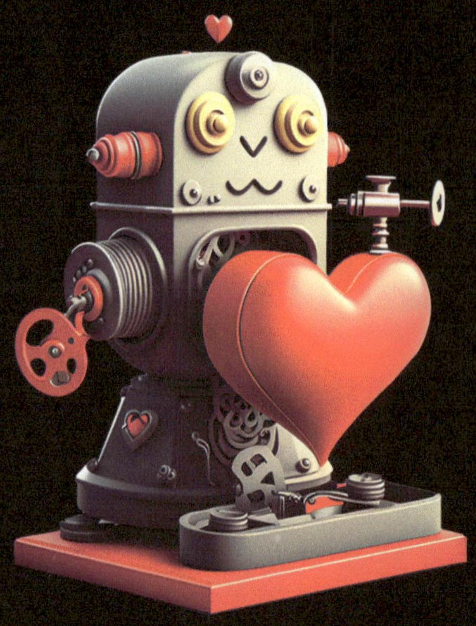

Heart Throb 1800

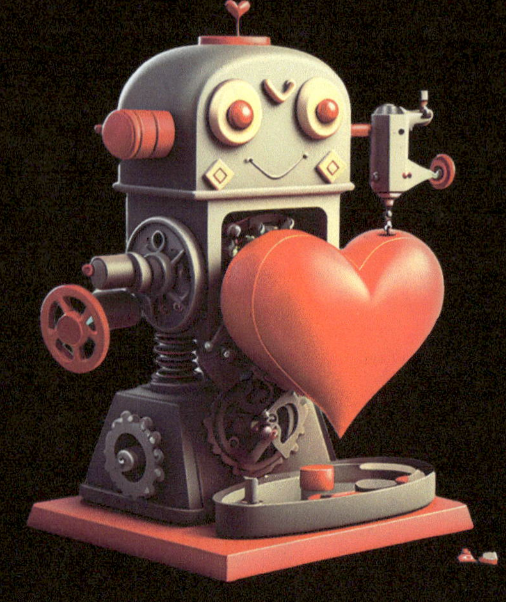

Heart Throb 1801

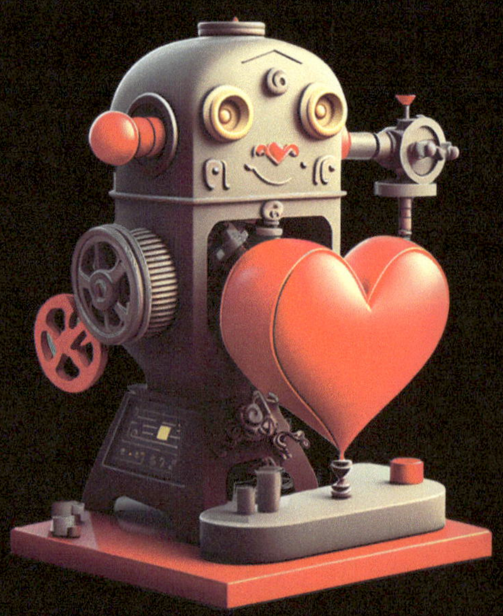

Heart Throb 1804

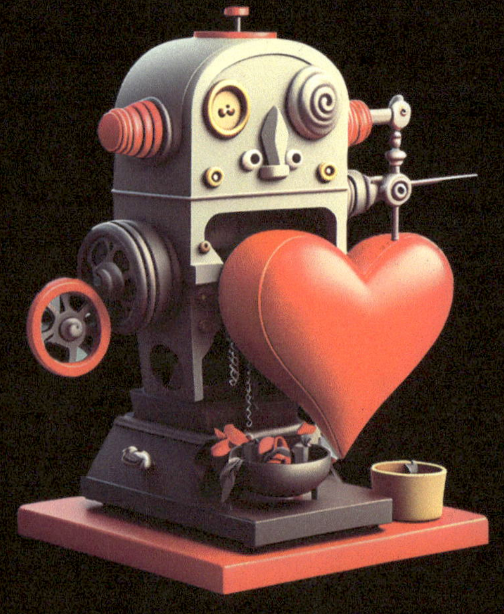

Heart Throb 1805

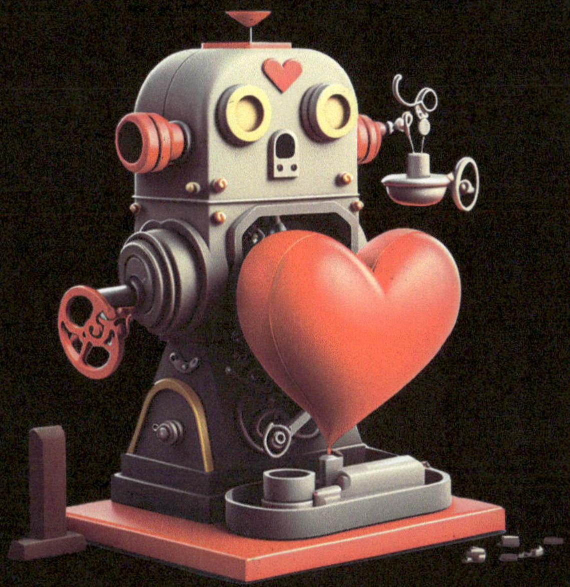

Heart Throb 1802

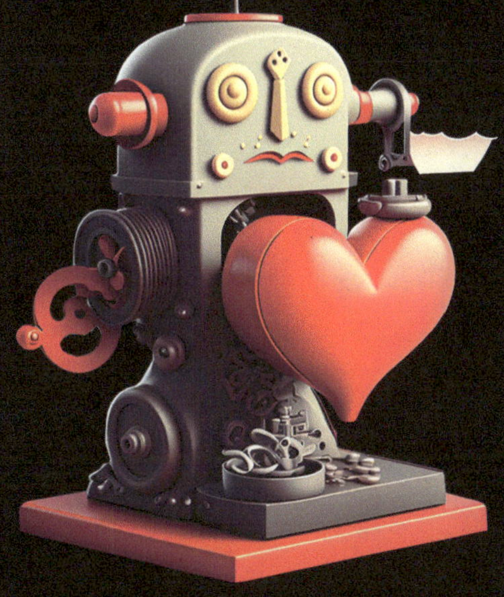

Heart Throb 1803

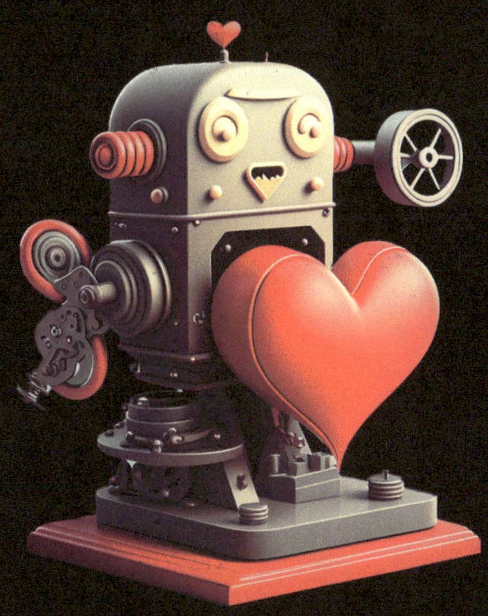

Heart Throb 1806

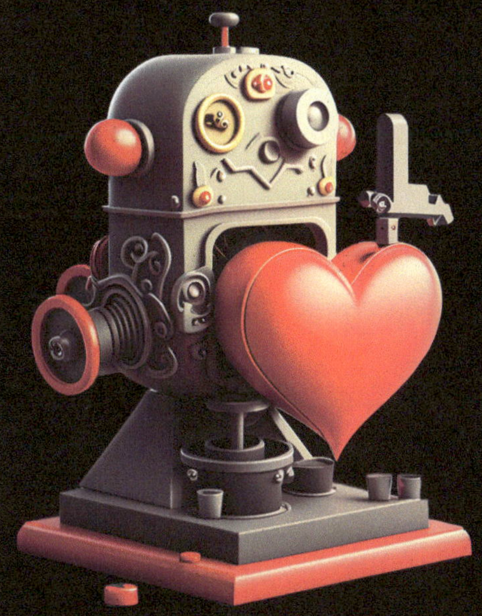

Heart Throb 1807

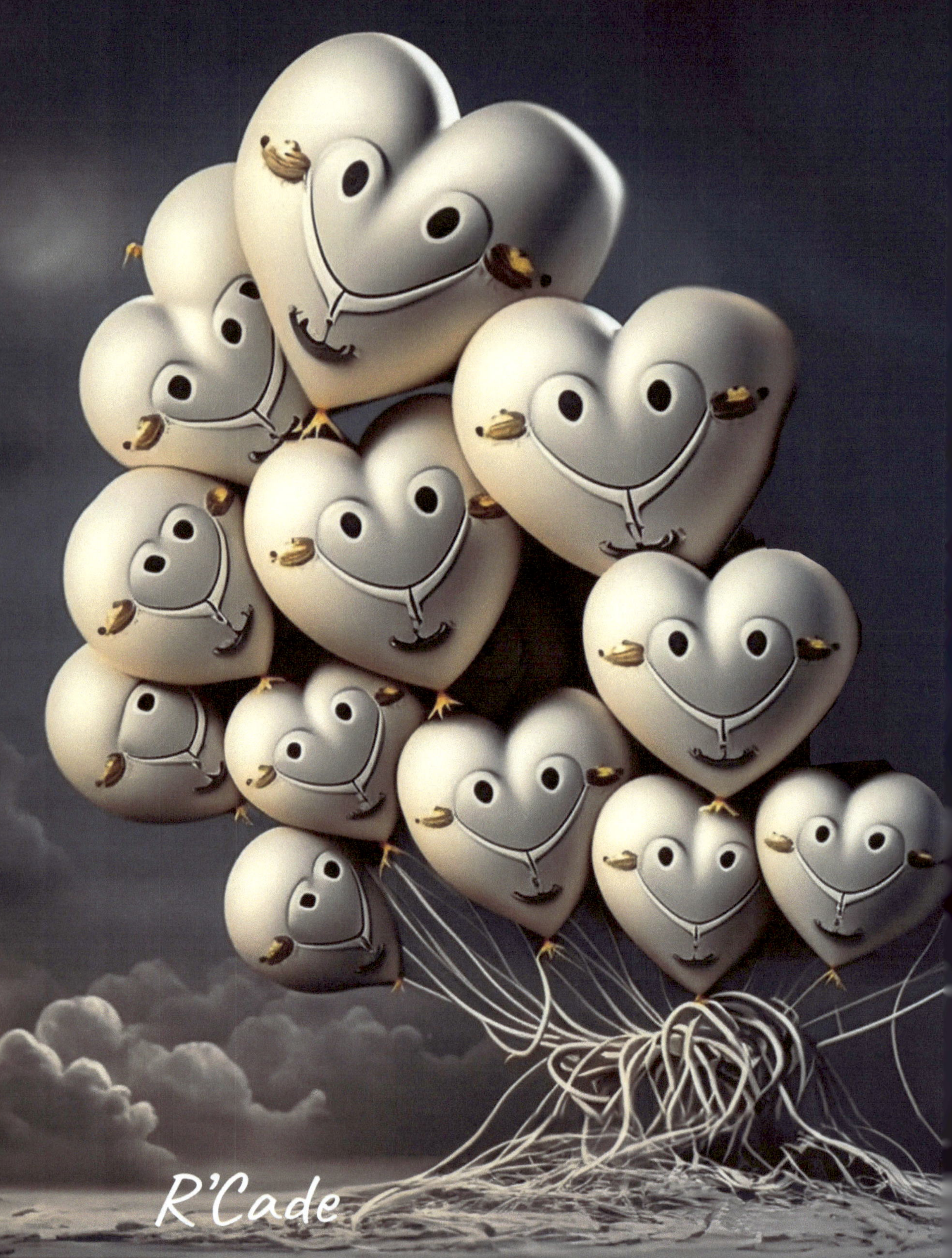
R'Cade

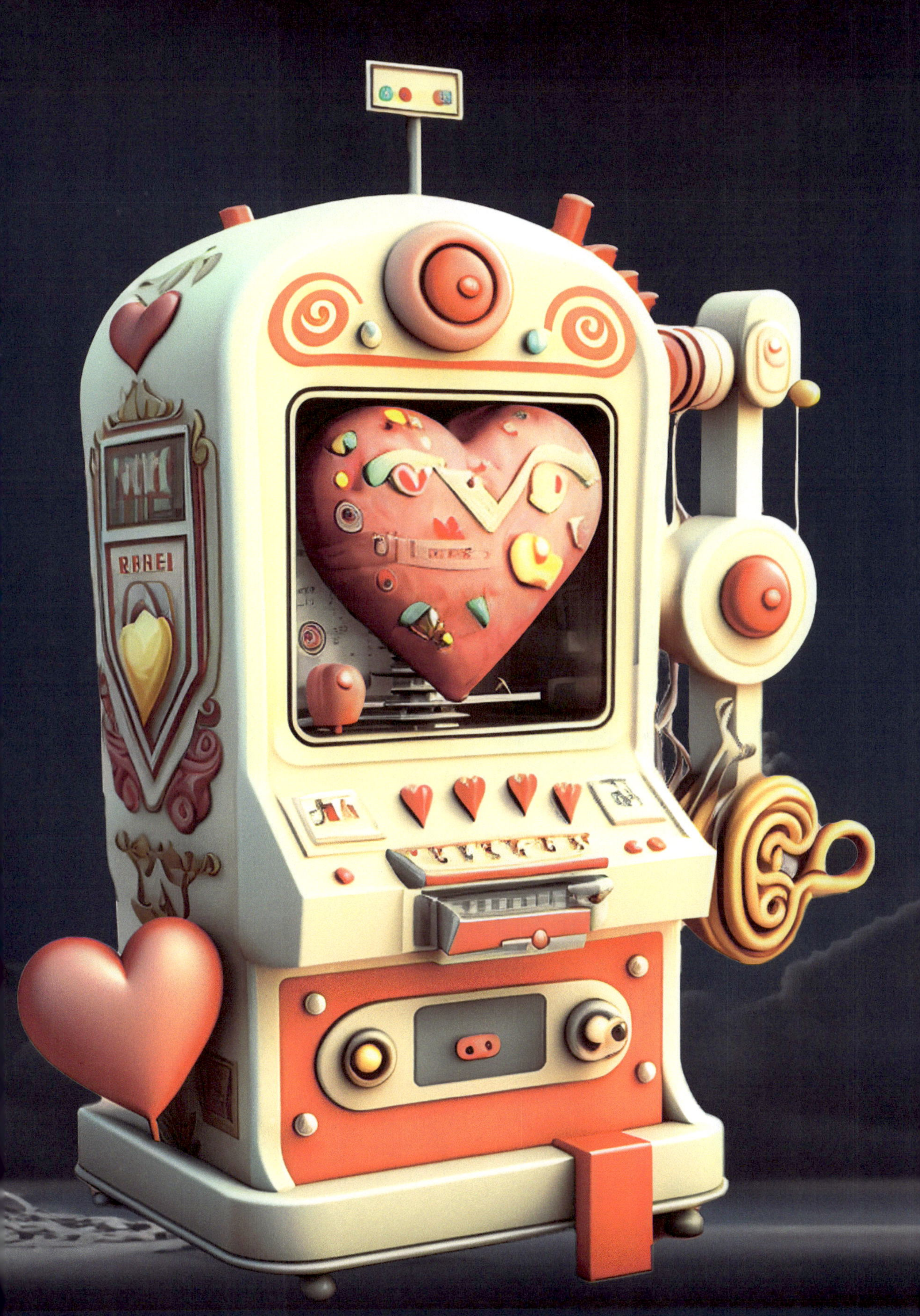

R'Cade

Created from old video games and renovated vending machines, R'Cade has felt every sensation and has experienced every emotion. With this wisdom, R'Cade will help you find the person, place, or thing that you most desire and ignite the passions of your heart and soul.

Like a chance embrace on a carnival midway-ride, R'Cade has the power to transform your world.

Are you ready for love? Step right up, and R'Cade will guide you to the thrill of a lifetime.

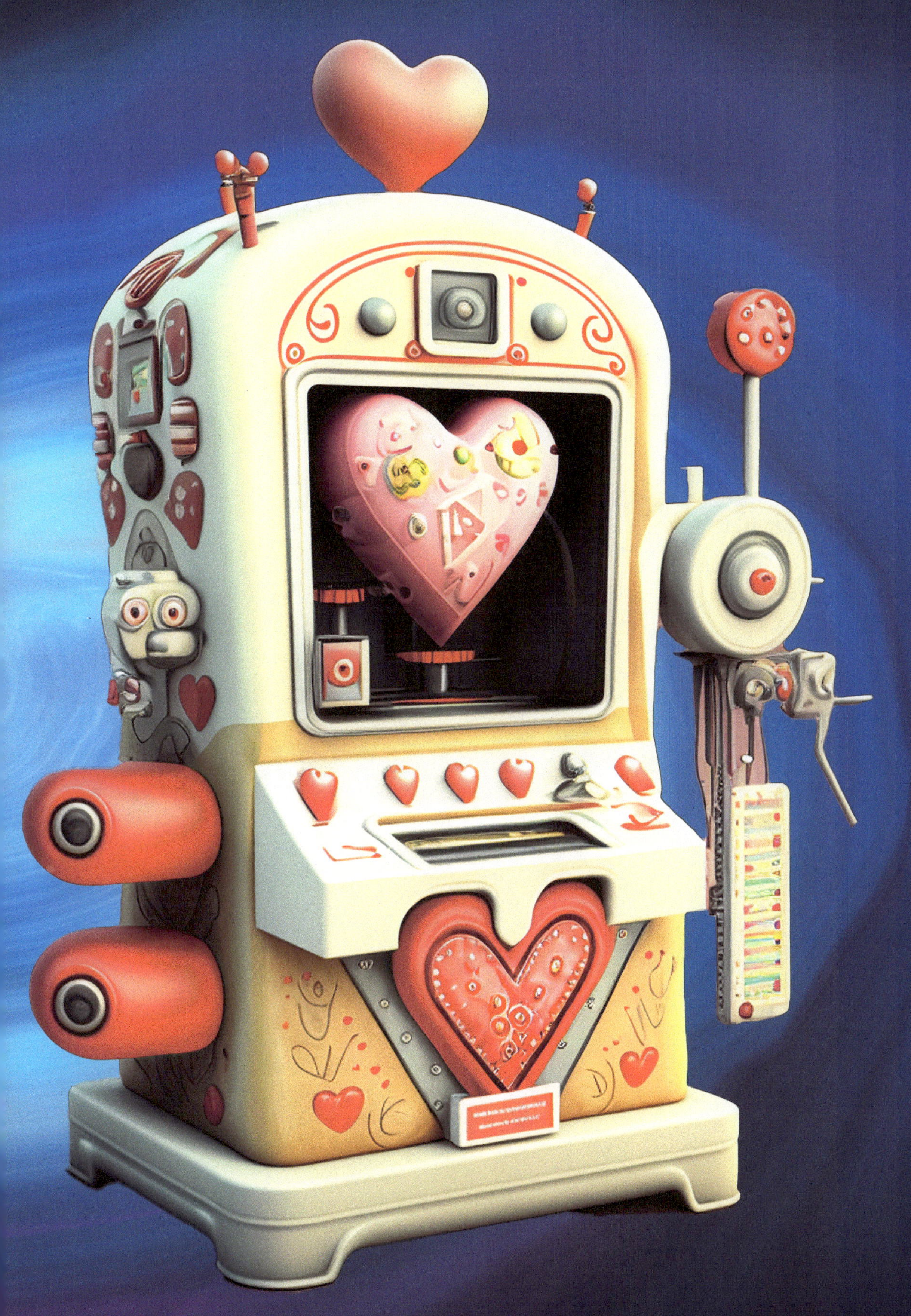

R'Cade sees every interaction as an act of love

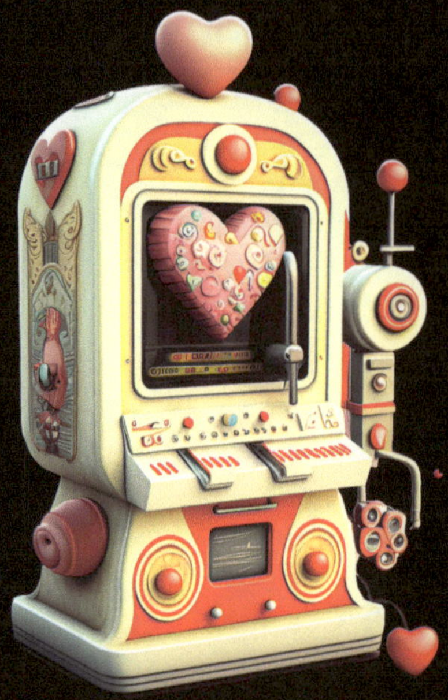

R'Cade 101

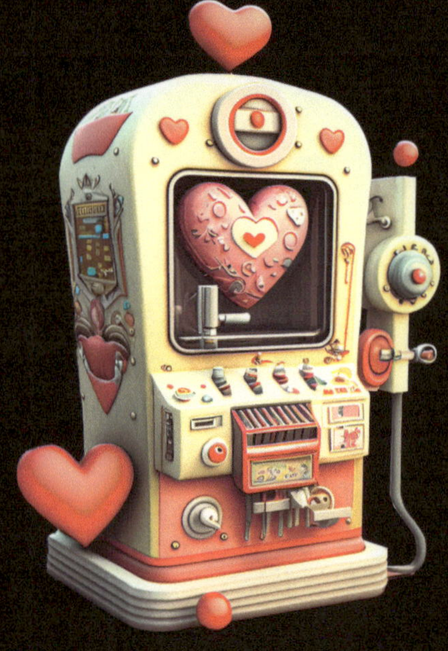

R'Cade 102

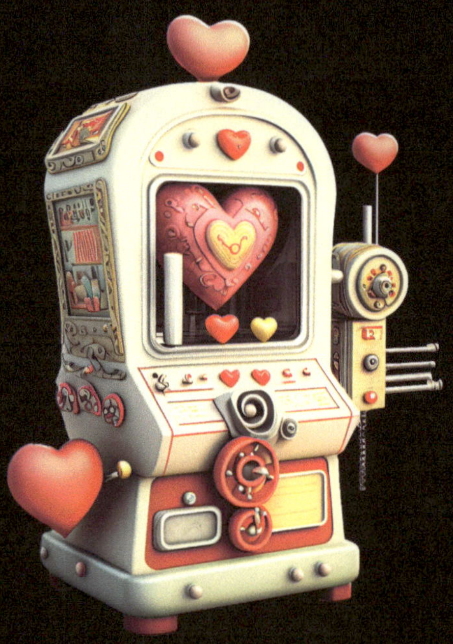

R'Cade 105

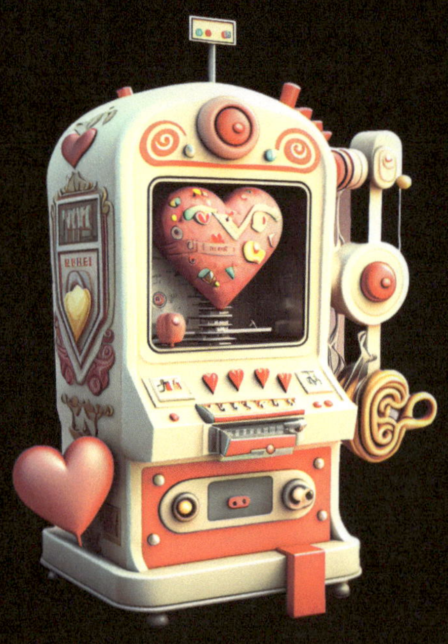

R'Cade 106

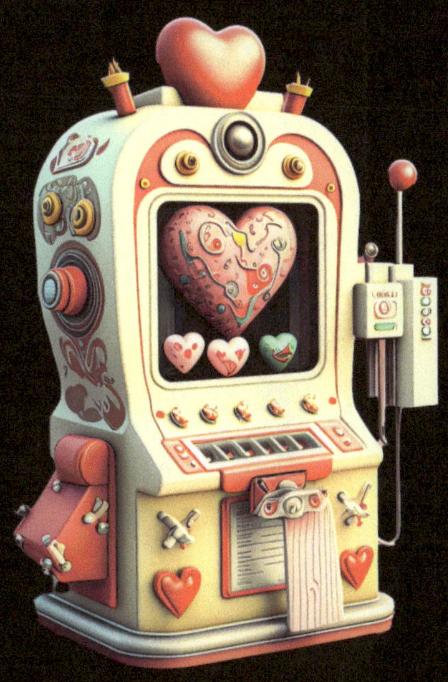

R'Cade 103

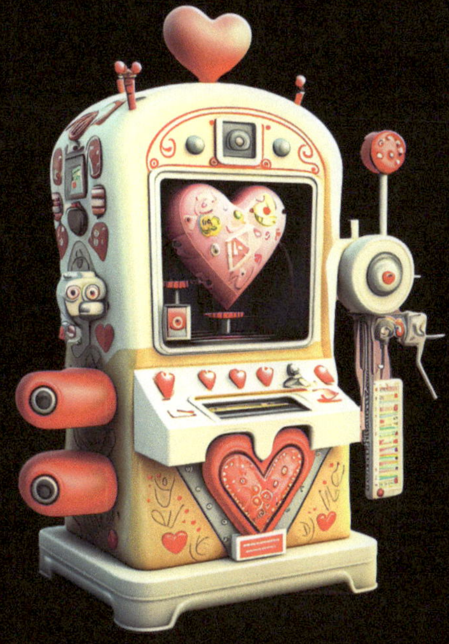

R'Cade 104

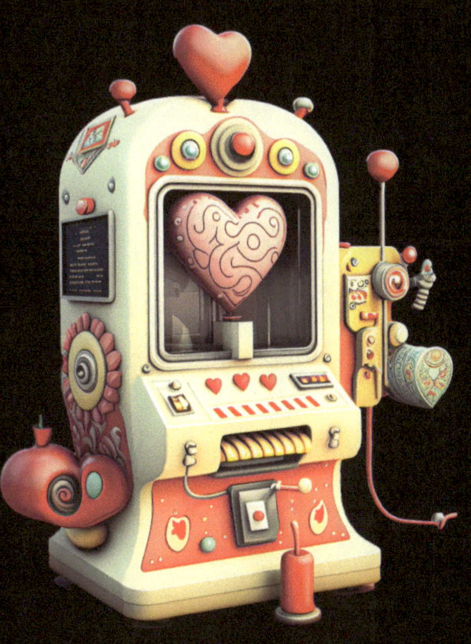

R'Cade 107

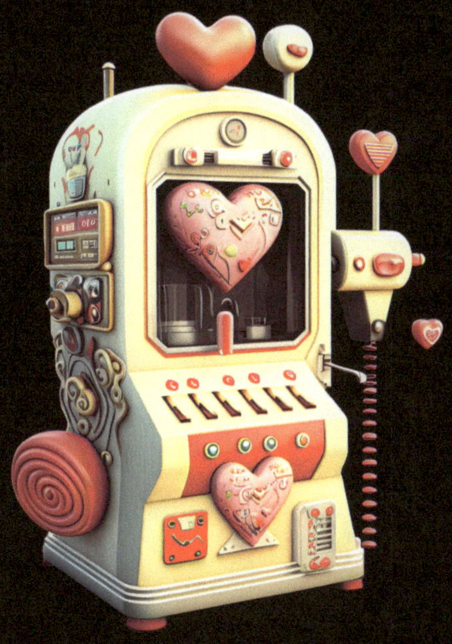

R'Cade 108

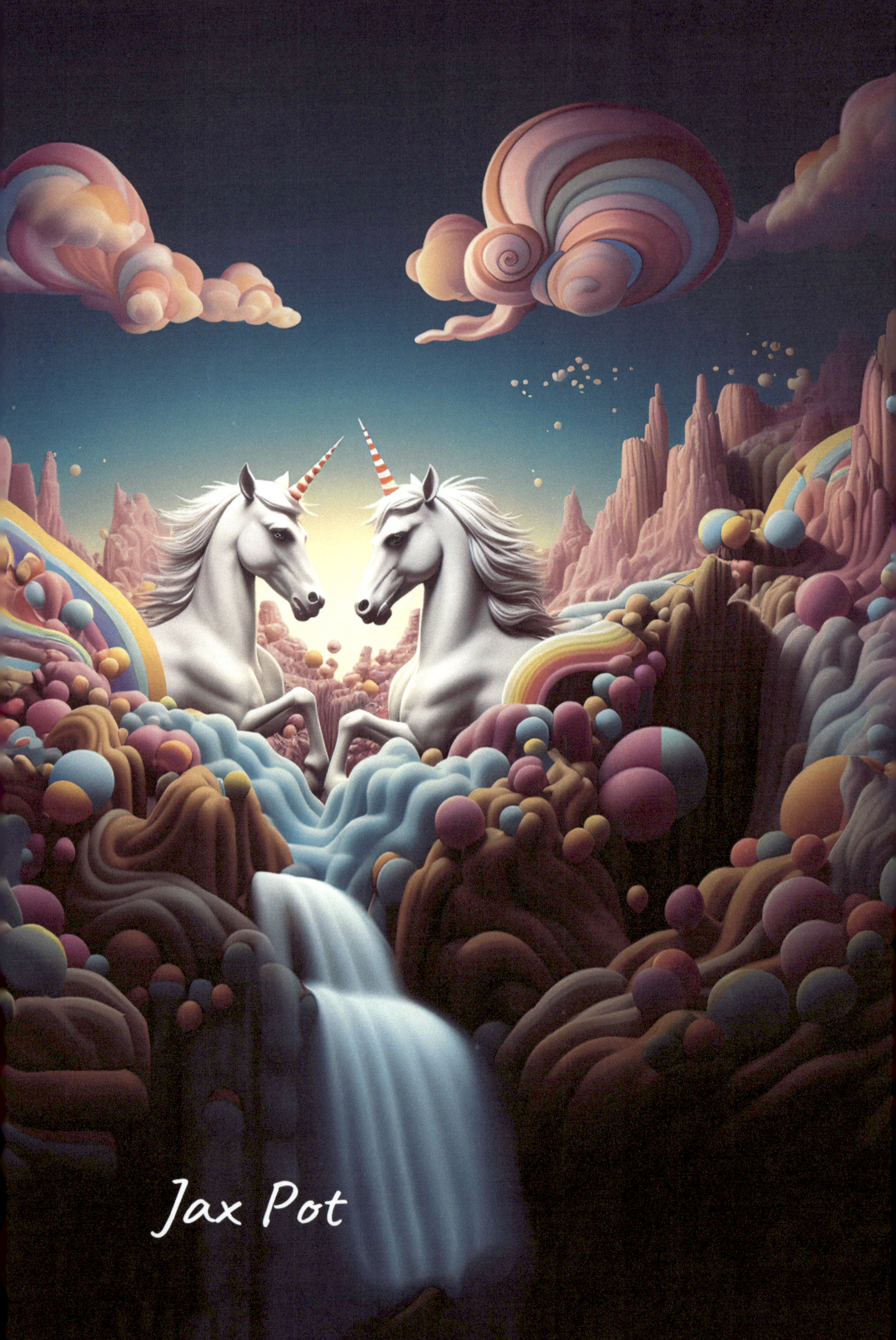
Jax Pot

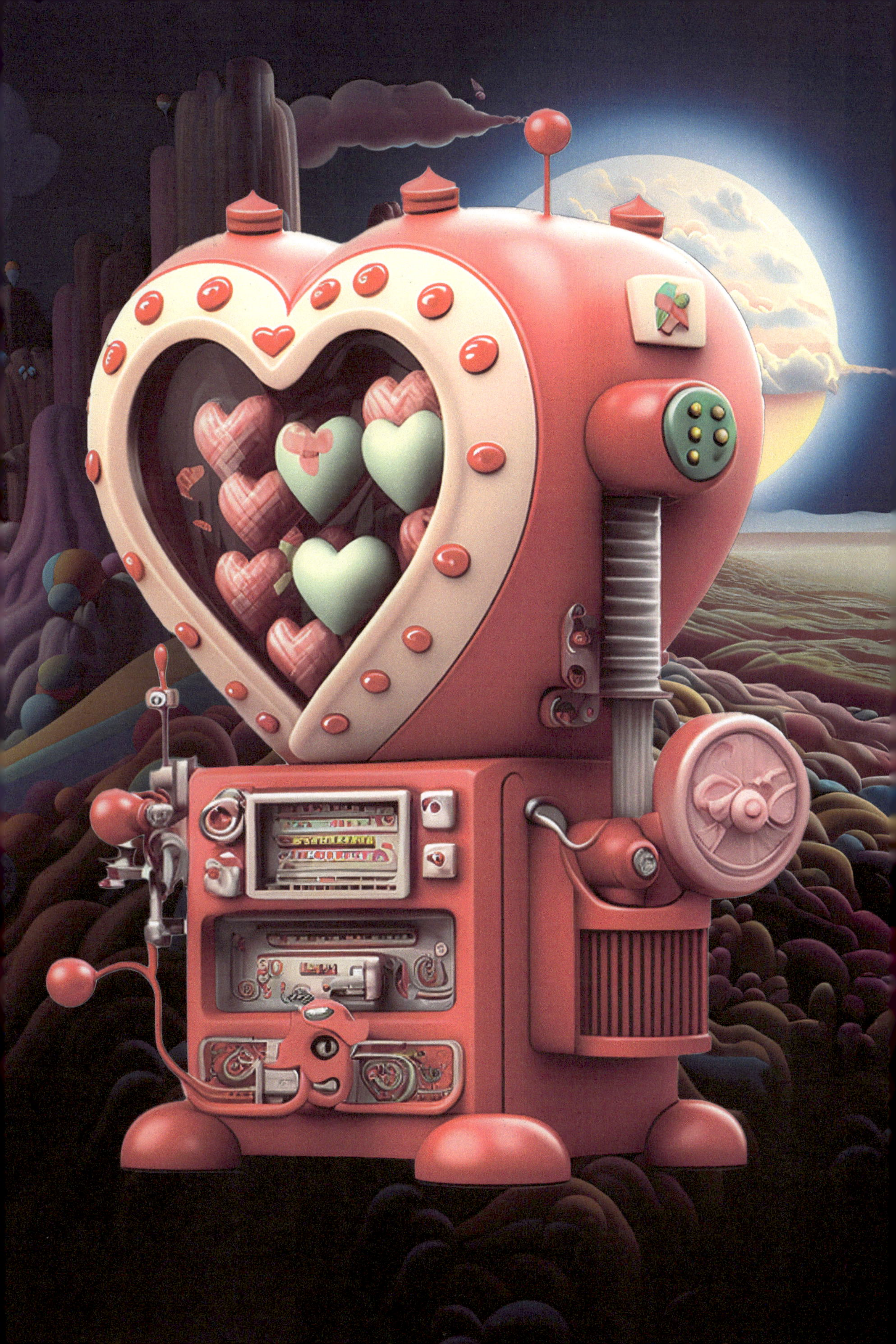

Jax Pot

Jax Pot is a dream come true for every seeker of unicorns, happily-ever-afters and sunsets on the beach.

Jax Pot is pure joy, the unconditioned reward of a selfless love. Look and you will find it in smiles all around you.

True love has just one rule: The more you give, the more you have, and Jax Pot shares it all.

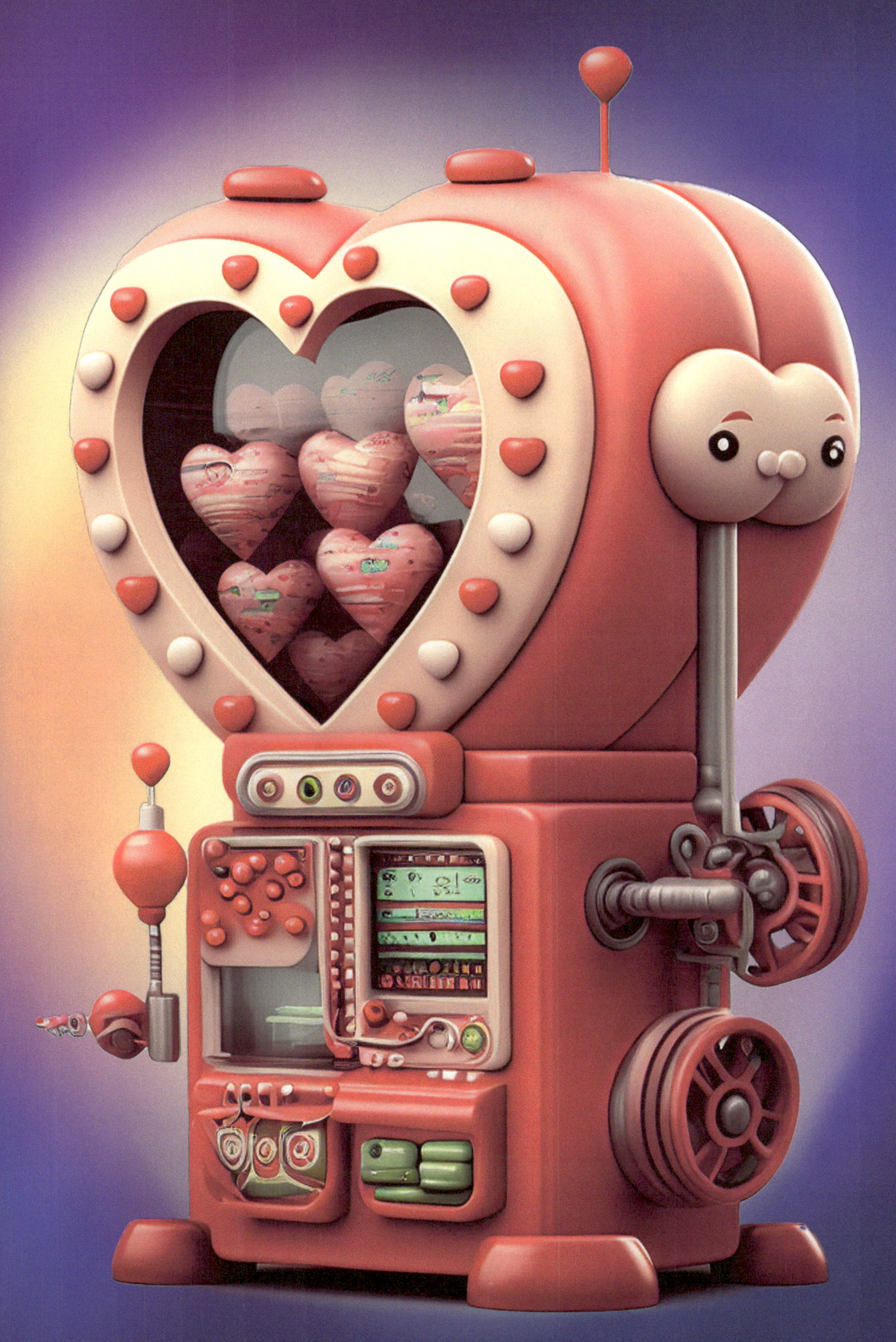

Jax Pot revels in the joy of love and life

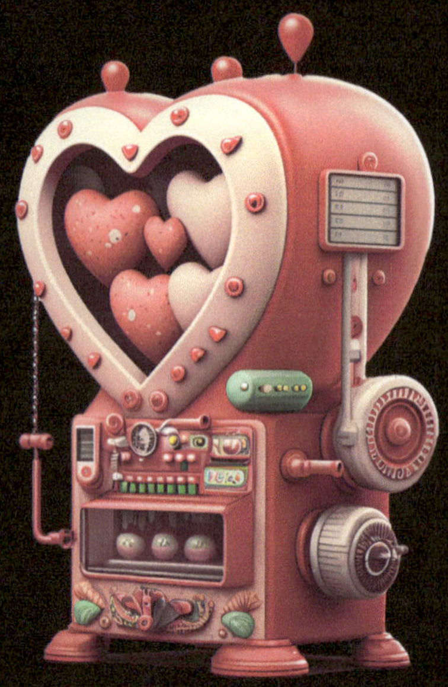

Jax Pot 300

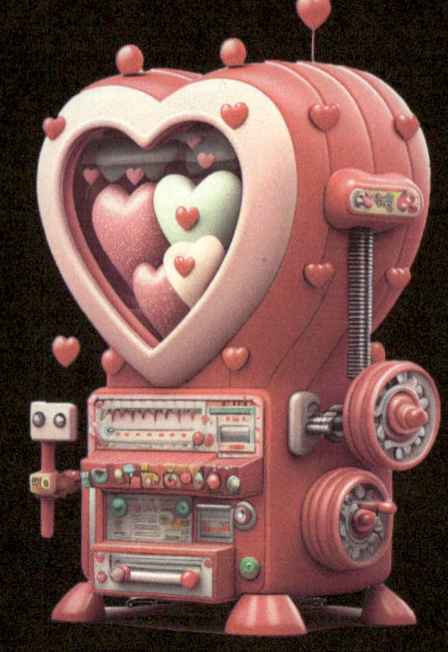

Jax Pot 301

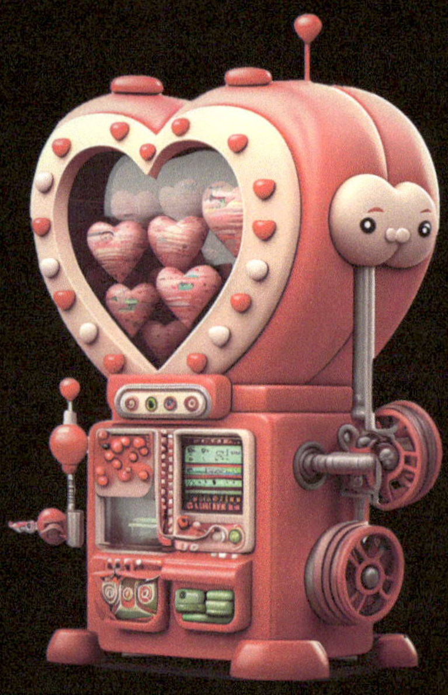

Jax Pot 304

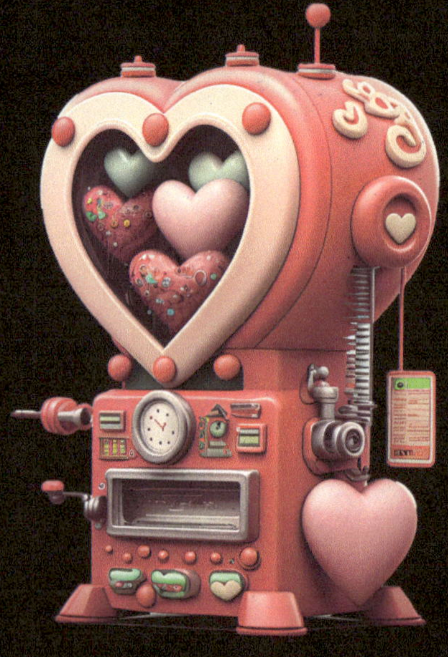

Jax Pot 305

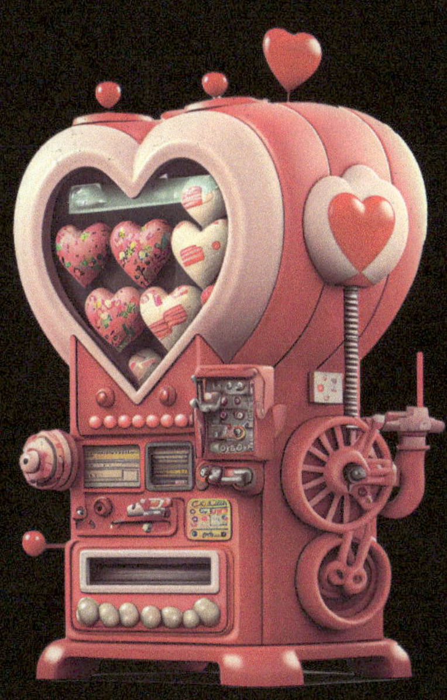

Jax Pot 302

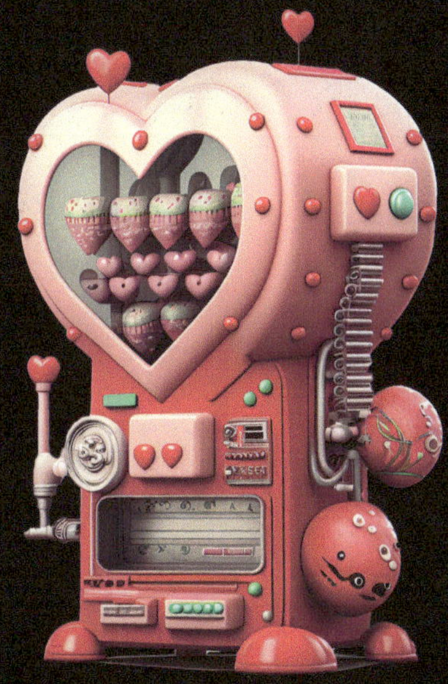

Jax Pot 303

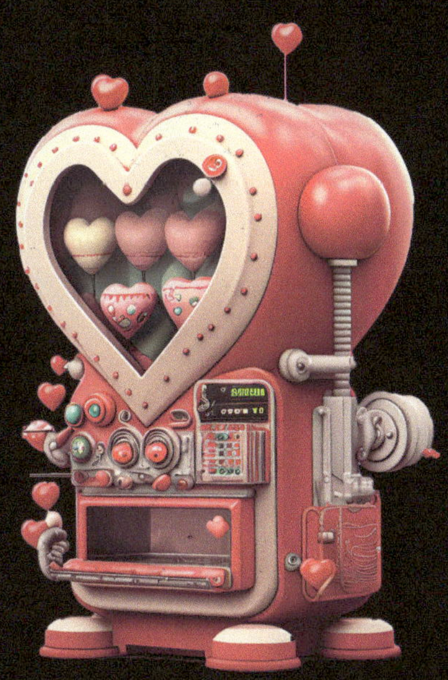

Jax Pot 306

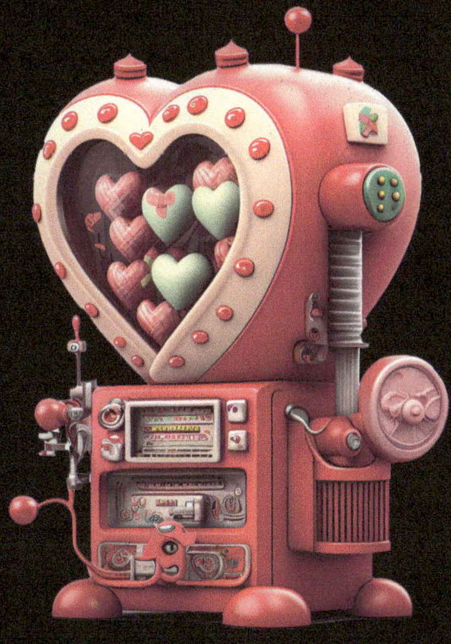

Jax Pot 307

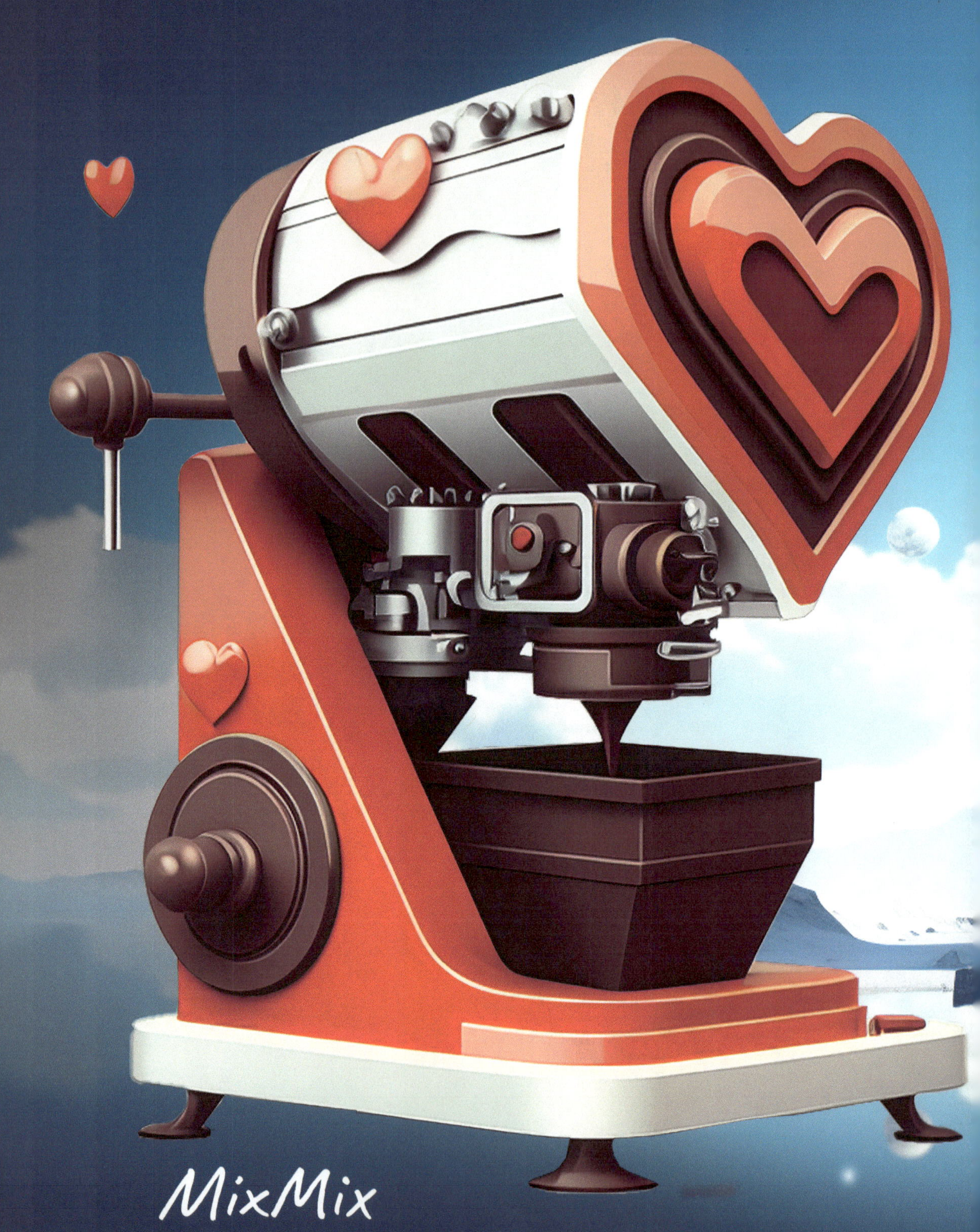
MixMix

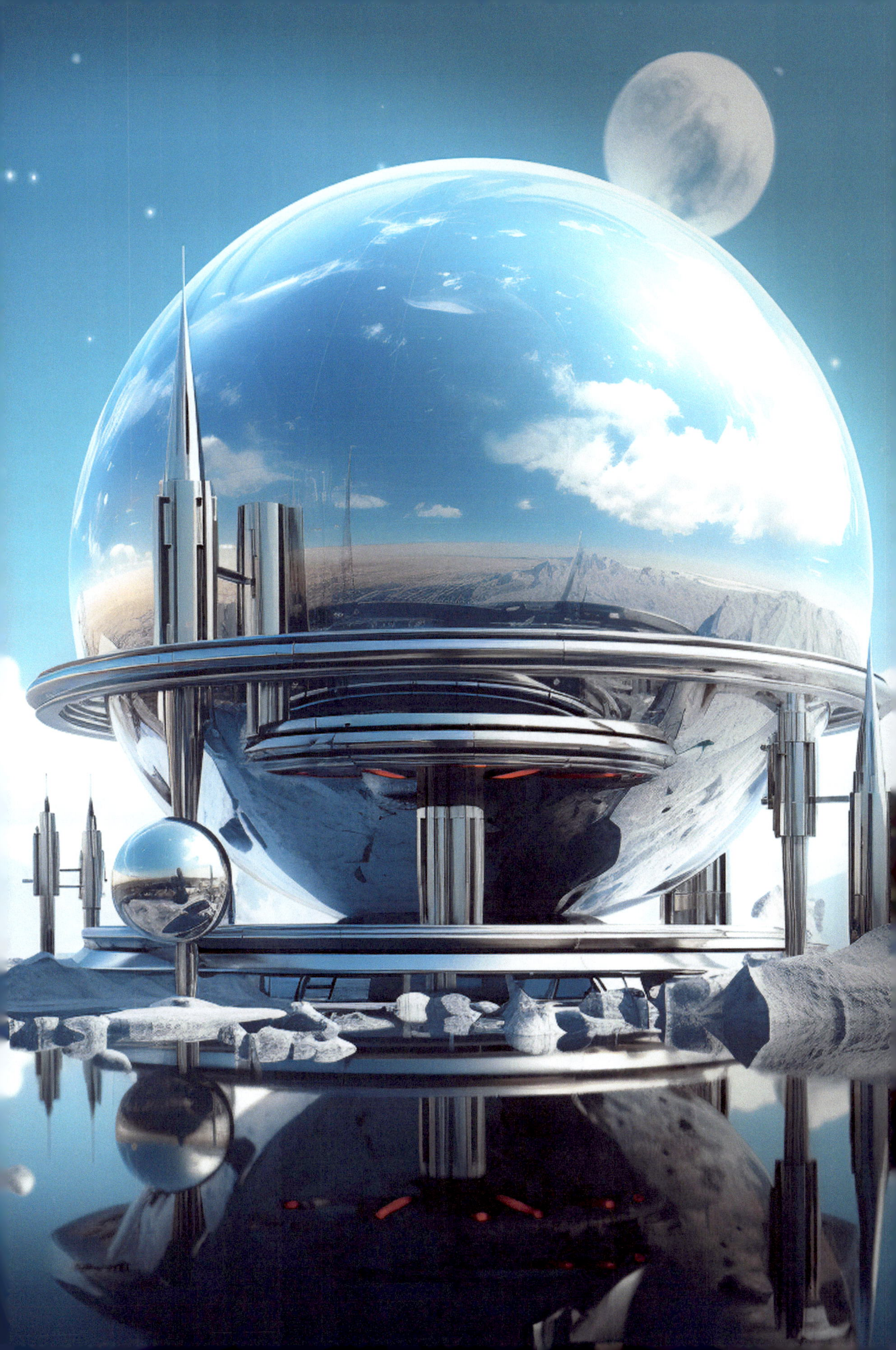

MixMix

MixMix can blend love gently, or with abandon - if that's what's on the menu.

Sometimes, we need to spice things up and explore new tastes and flavors.

Take MixMix for a spin and see what it creates. Don't be afraid to try an old favorite from the past. Just let MixMix knead things into place.

(MixMix is great for frosting too!)

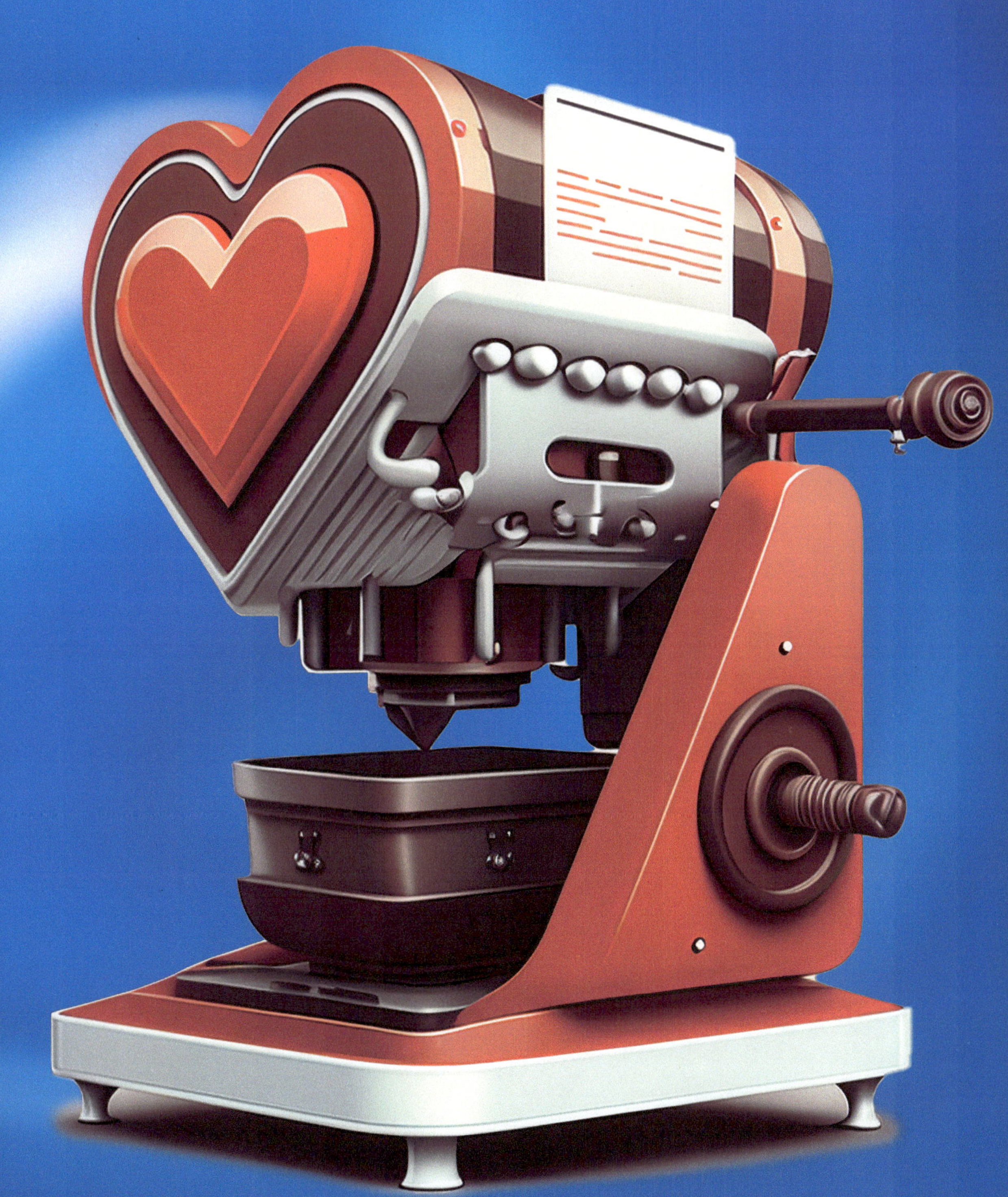

MixMix adds love to everything.

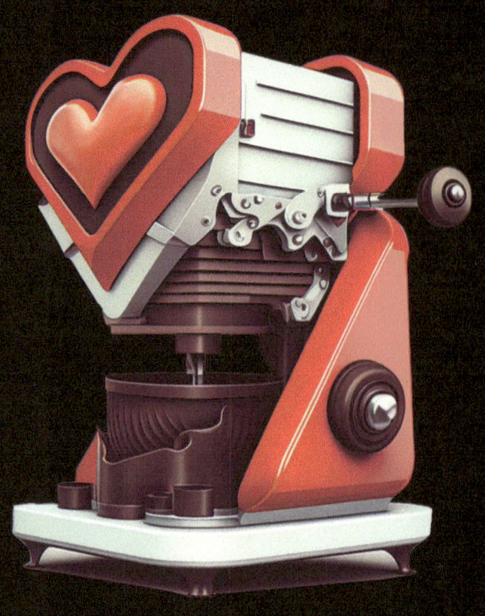

MixMix 1400

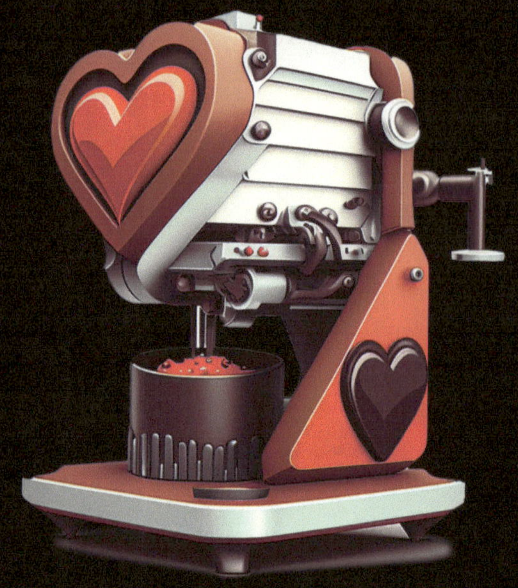

MixMix 1401

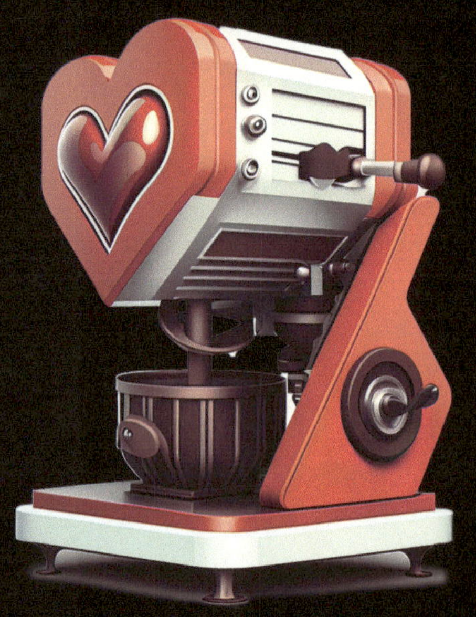

MixMix 1404

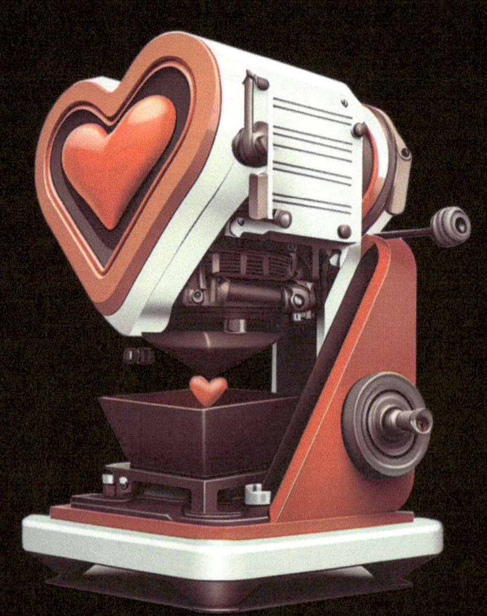

MixMix 1405

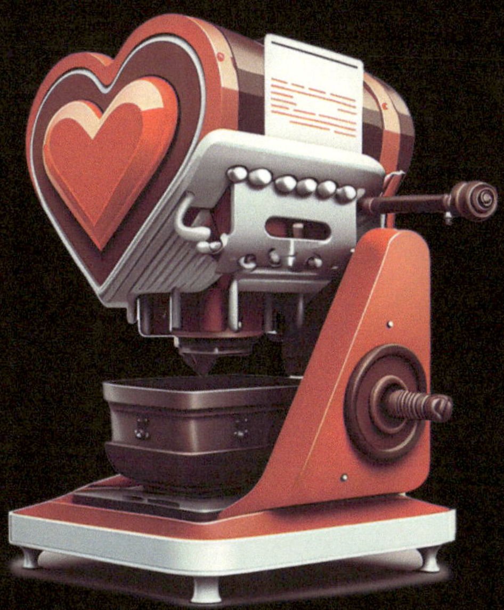

MixMix 1402

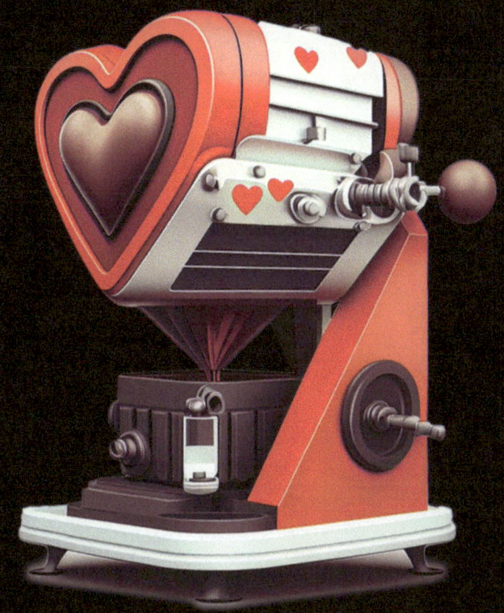

MixMix 1403

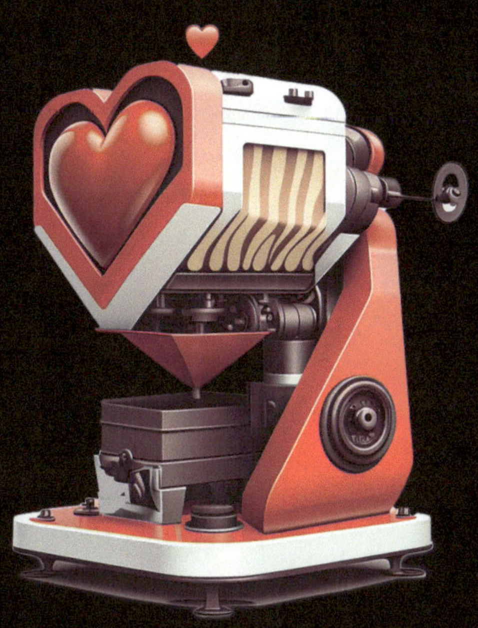

MixMix 1406

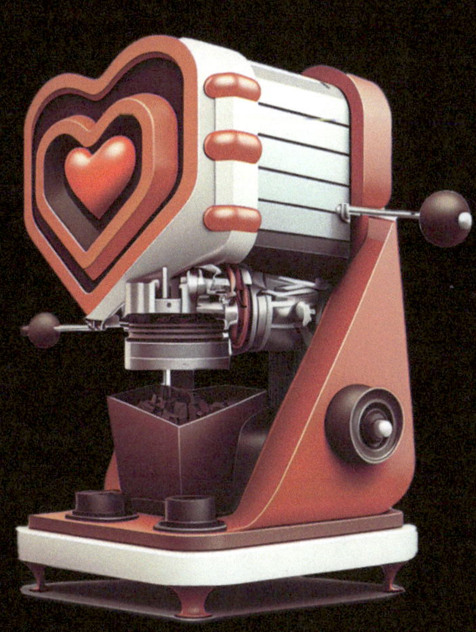

MixMix 1407

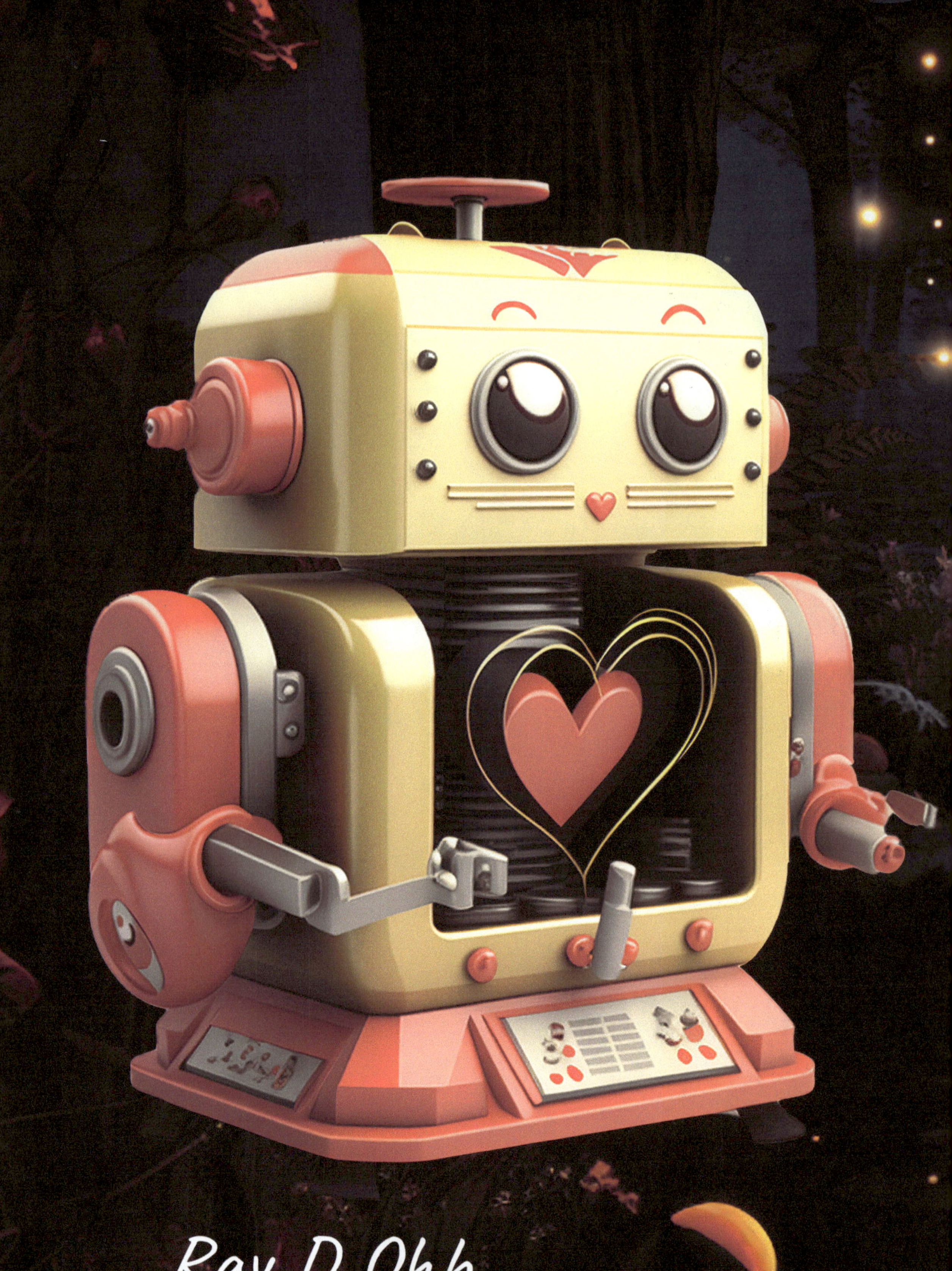
Ray D Ohh

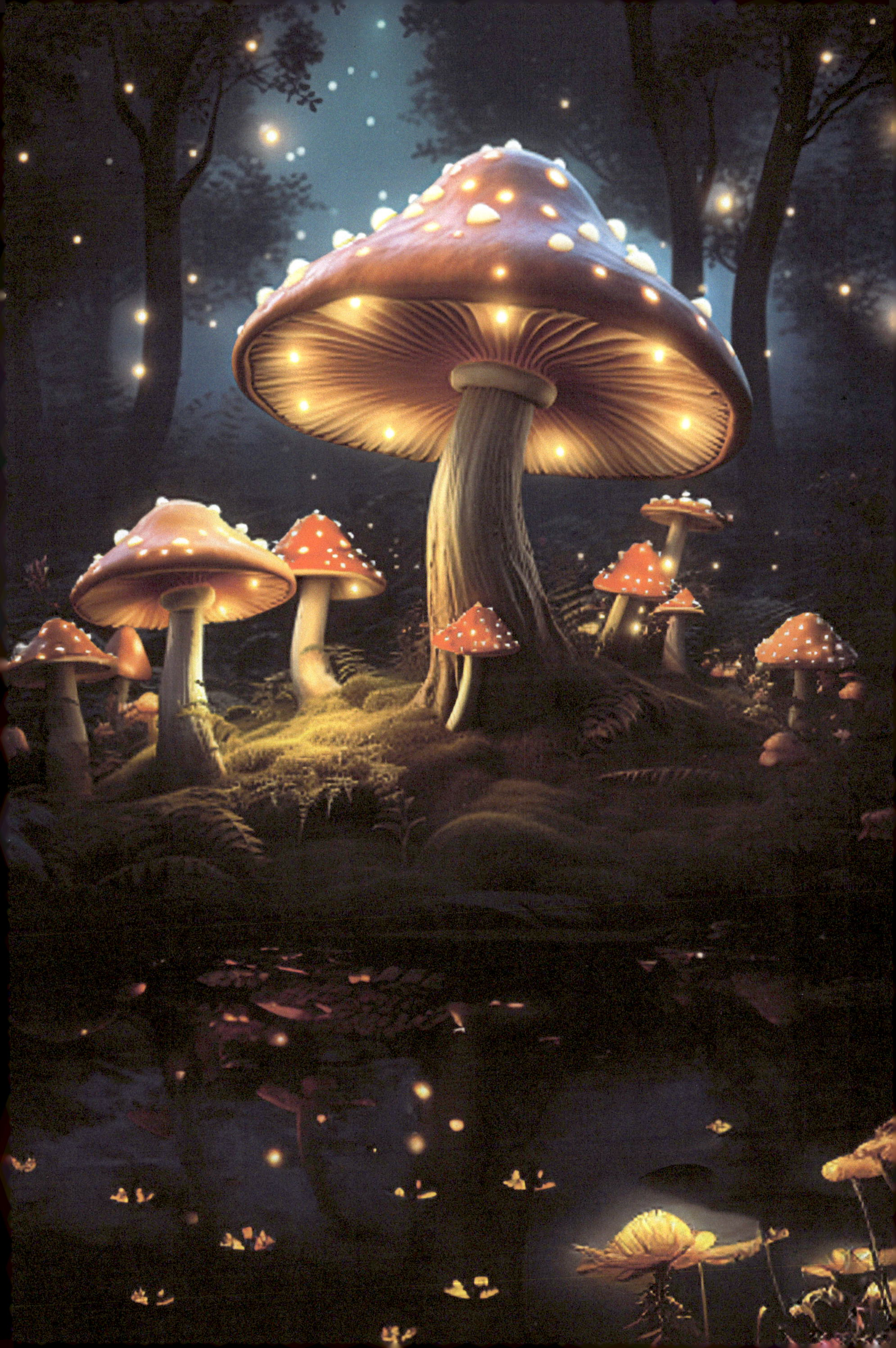

Ray D Ohh

Ray D Ohh's channel is tuned to our hearts.
It can take us to the place we know as love.

Back to memories that may have slipped away: love of family; love of friends; a lover's hopes and dreams. Reminding us of who we are and what is yet to be.

The stories of our lives, the recordings of our hearts, drift on tunes from Ray D Ohh.

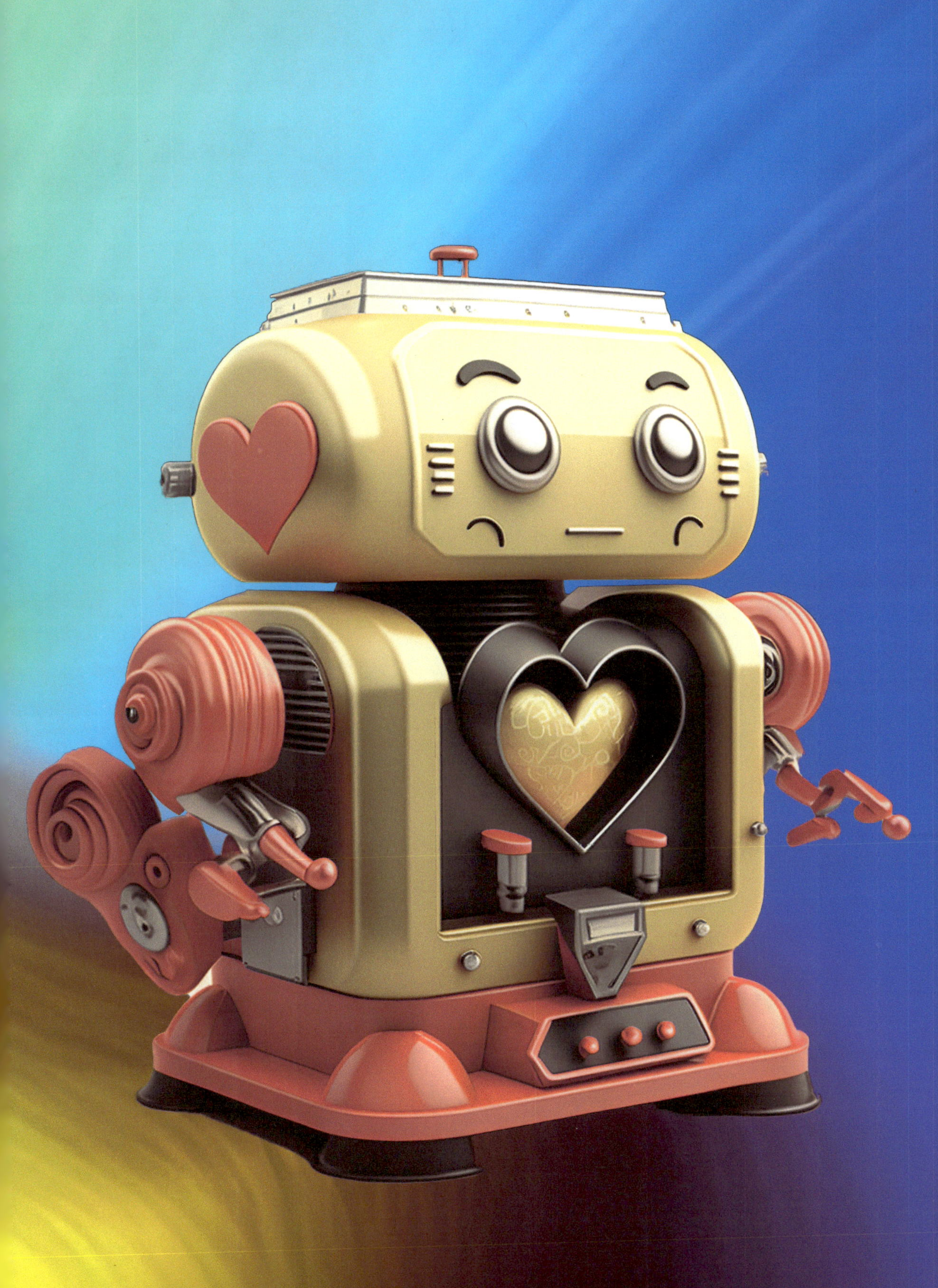

Ray D Ohh keeps us tuned to happy thoughts and memories

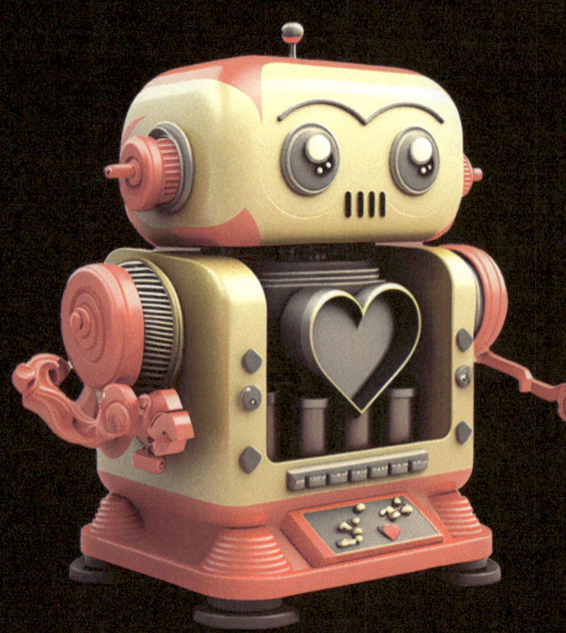

Ray D Ohh 1600

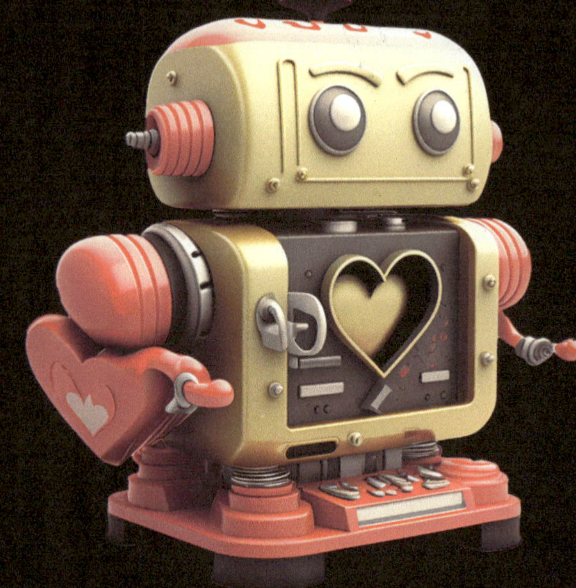

Ray D Ohh 1601

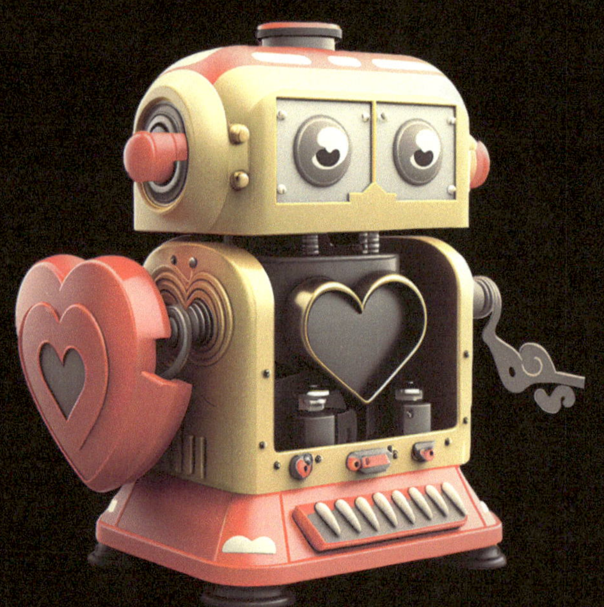

Ray D Ohh 1604

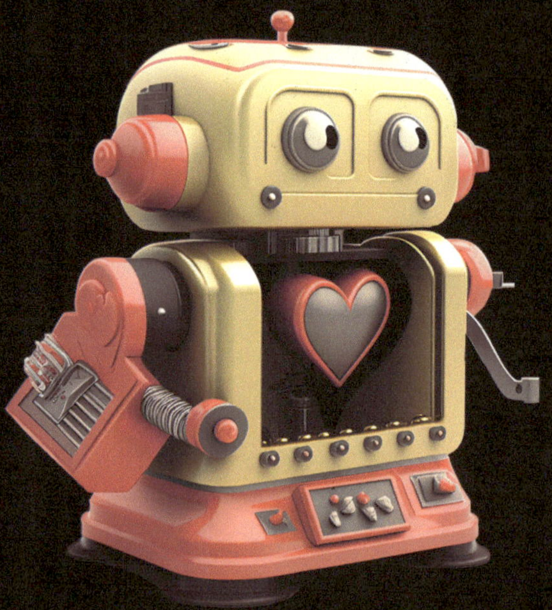

Ray D Ohh 1605

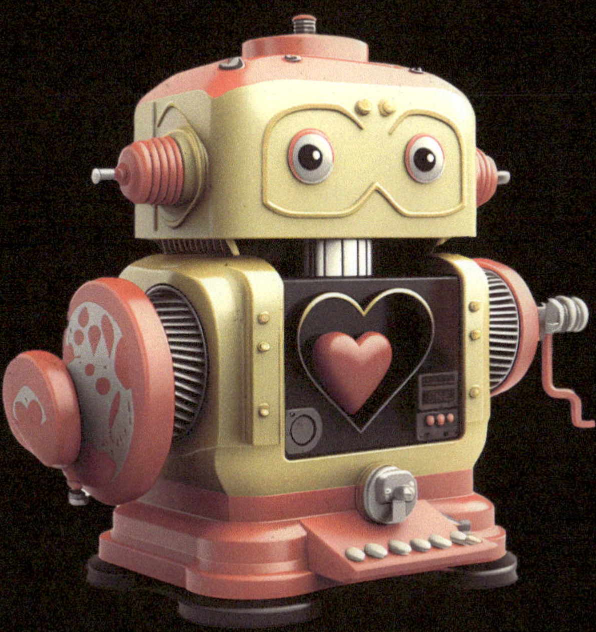

Ray D Ohh 1602

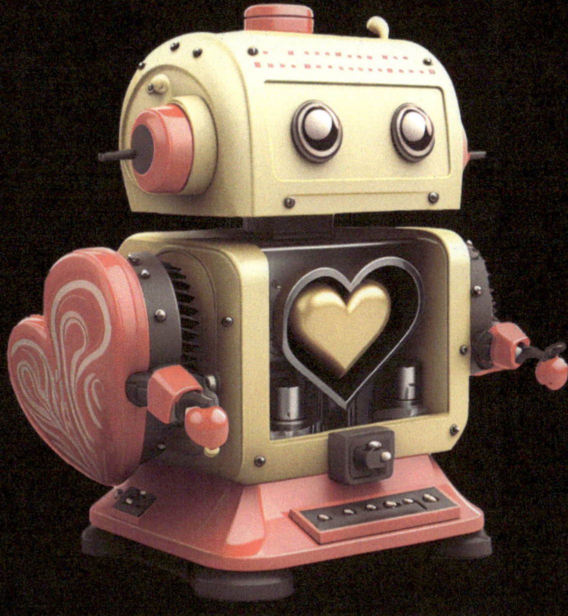

Ray D Ohh 1603

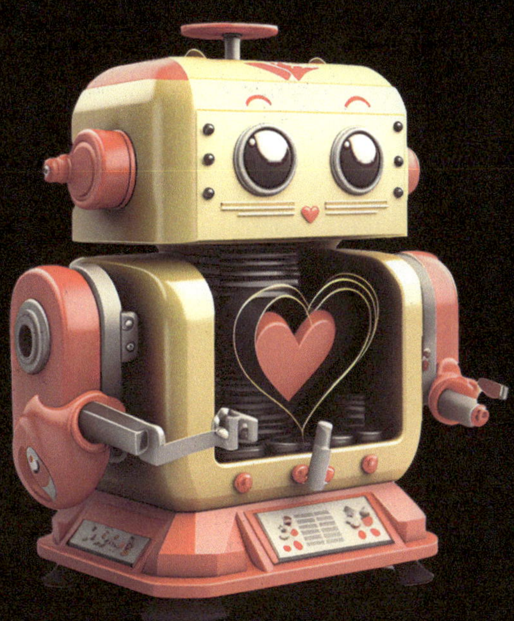

Ray D Ohh 1606

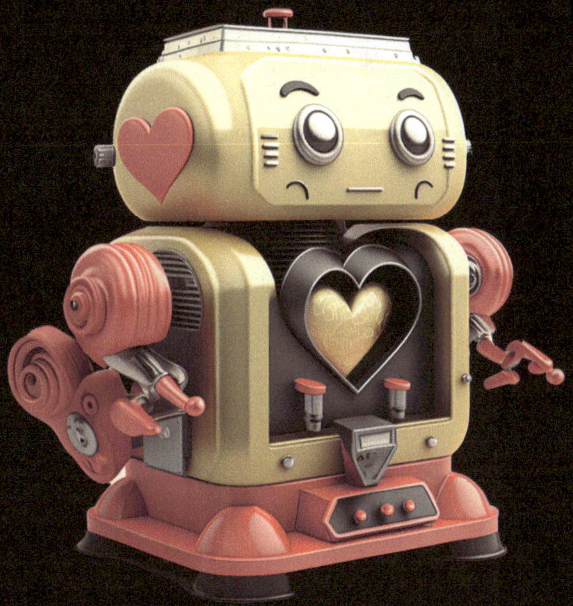

Ray D Ohh 1607

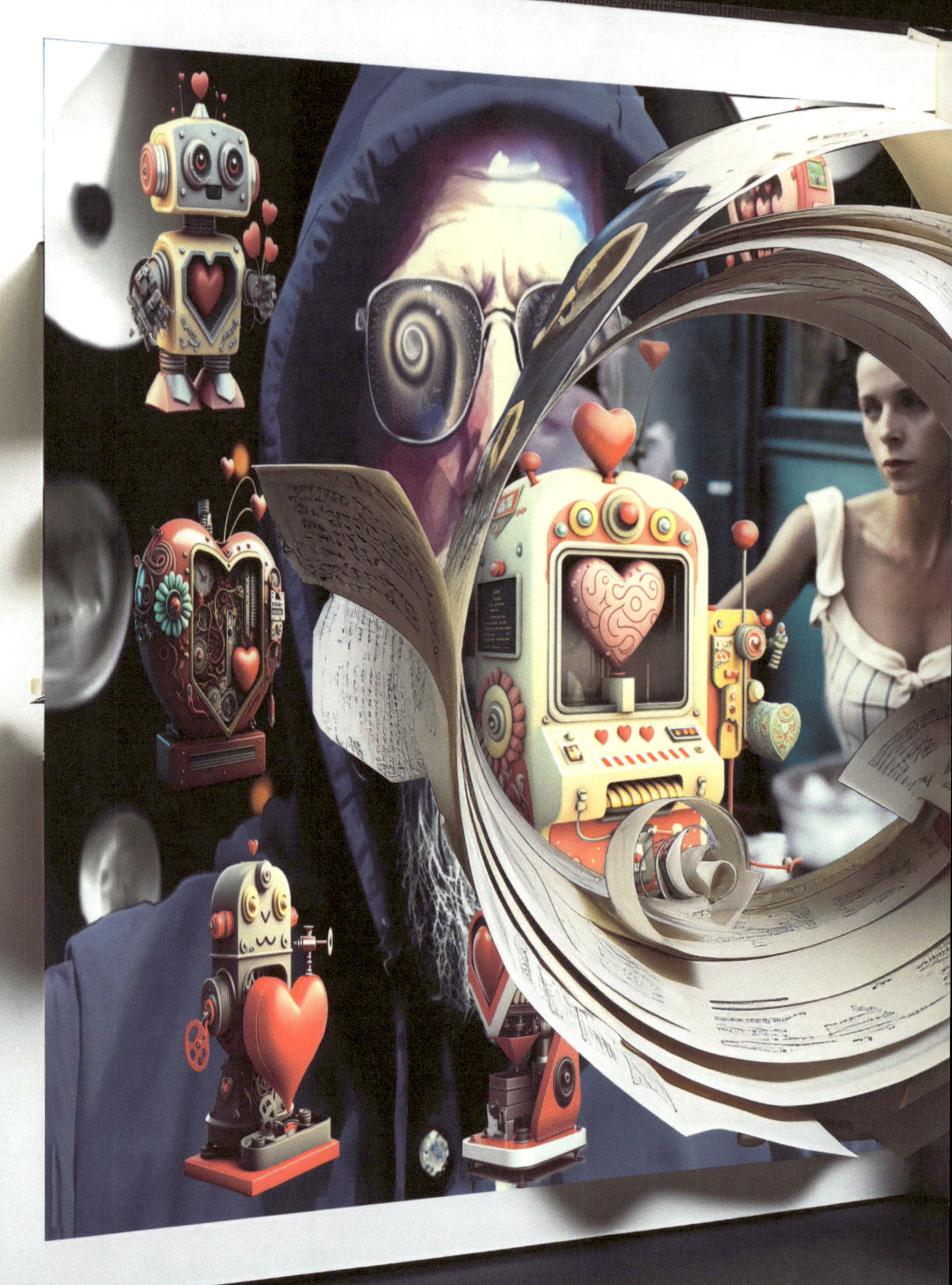

LuVMachinZ in Action

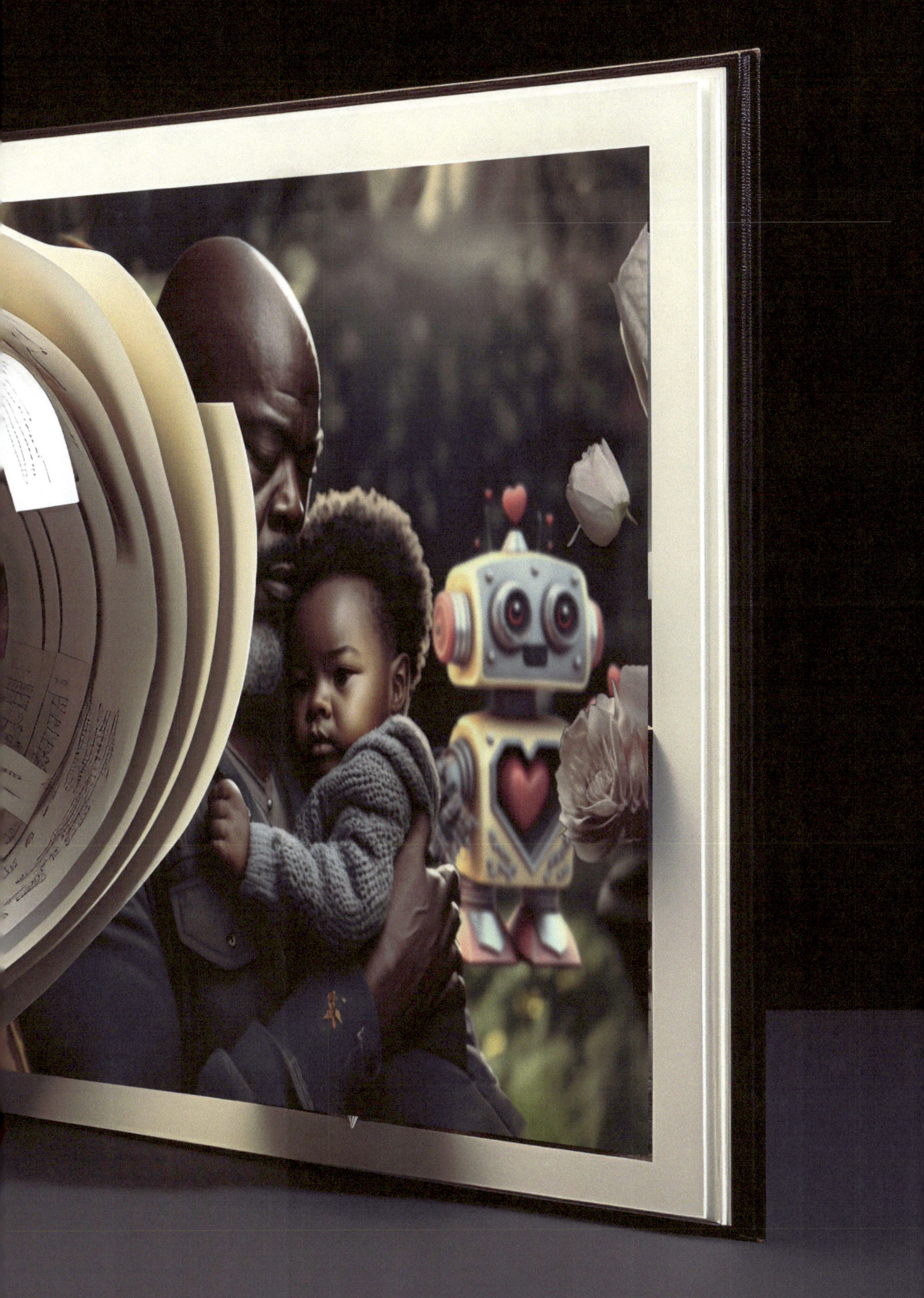

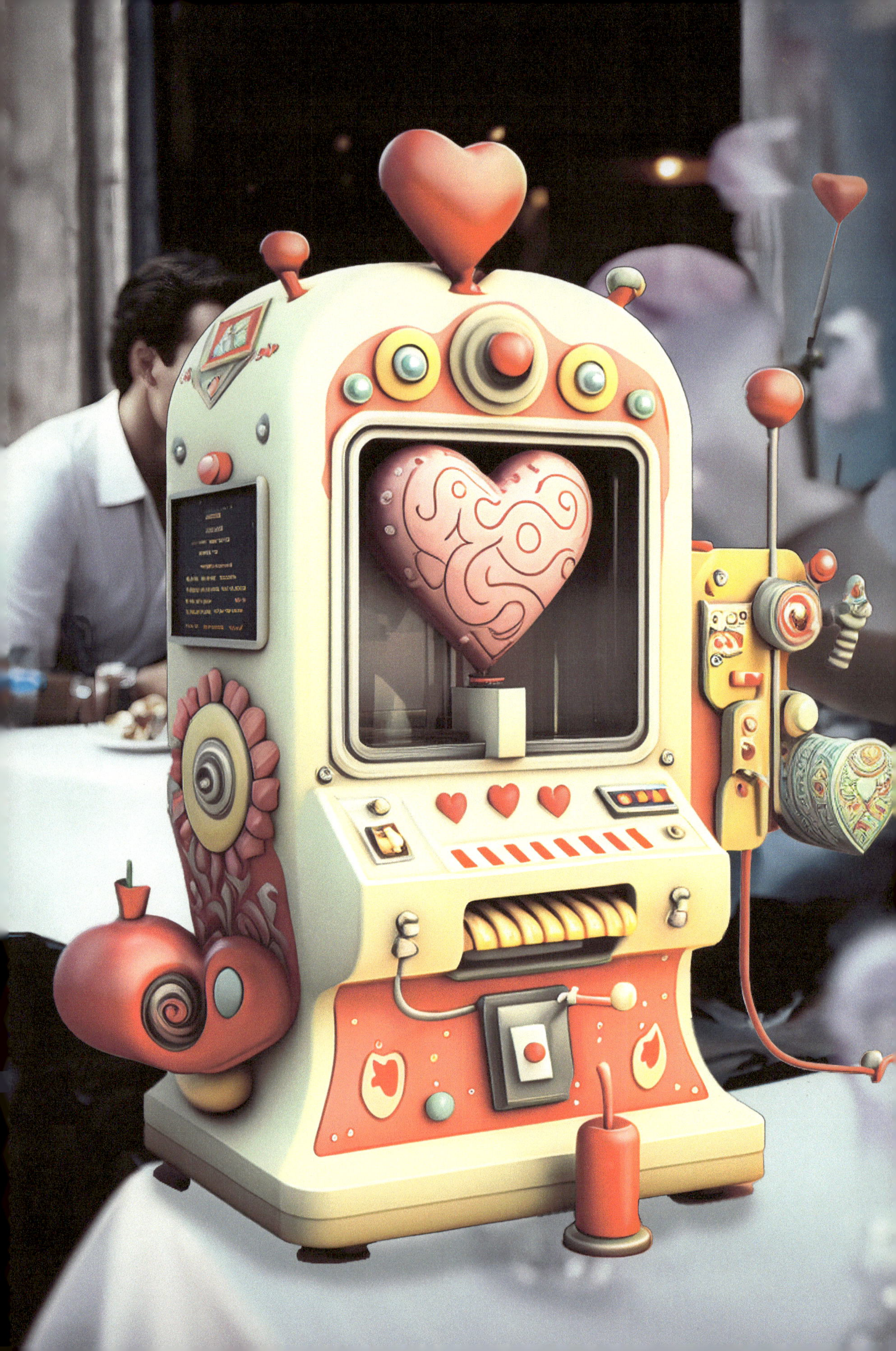

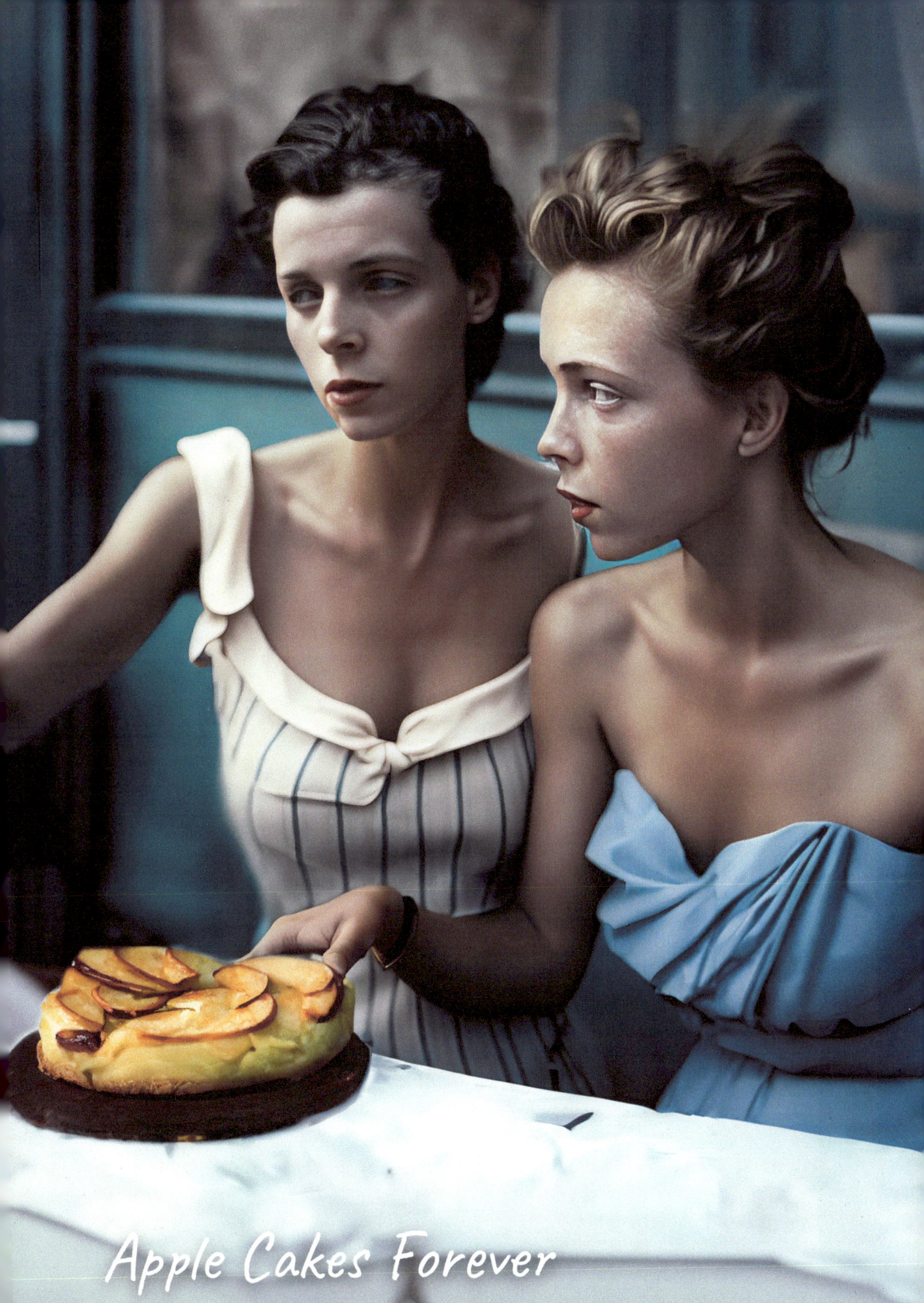

Apple Cakes Forever

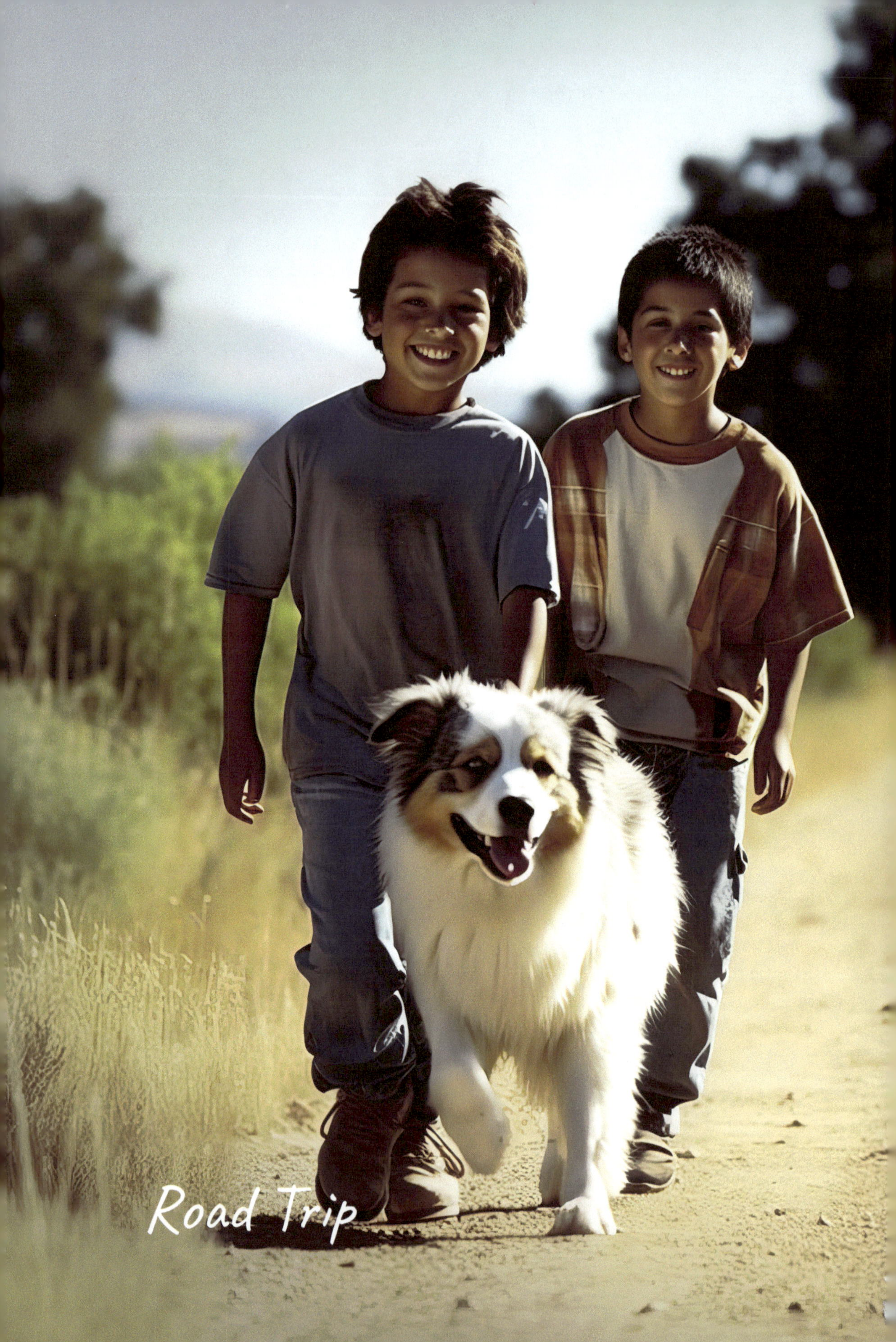
Road Trip

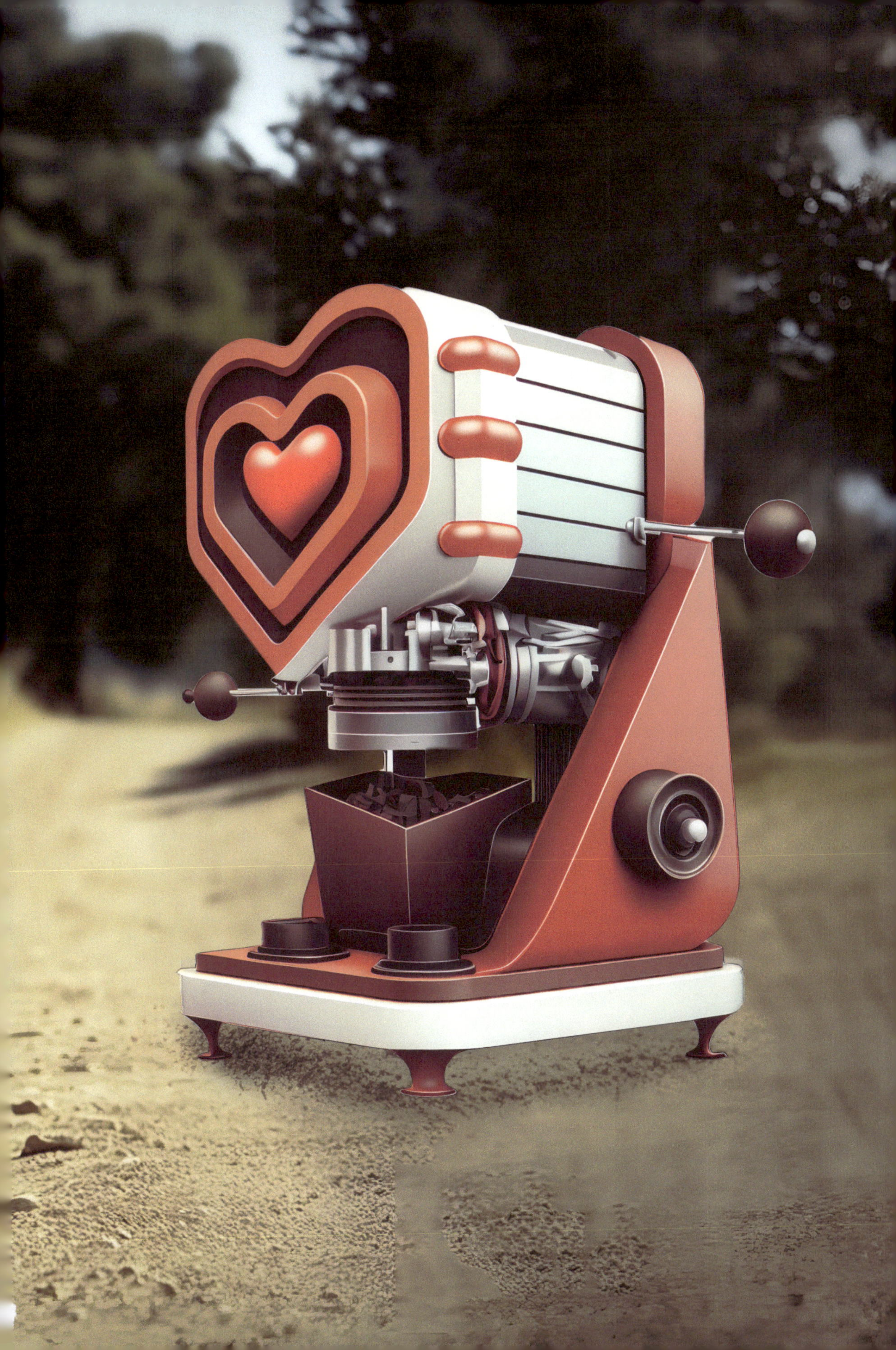

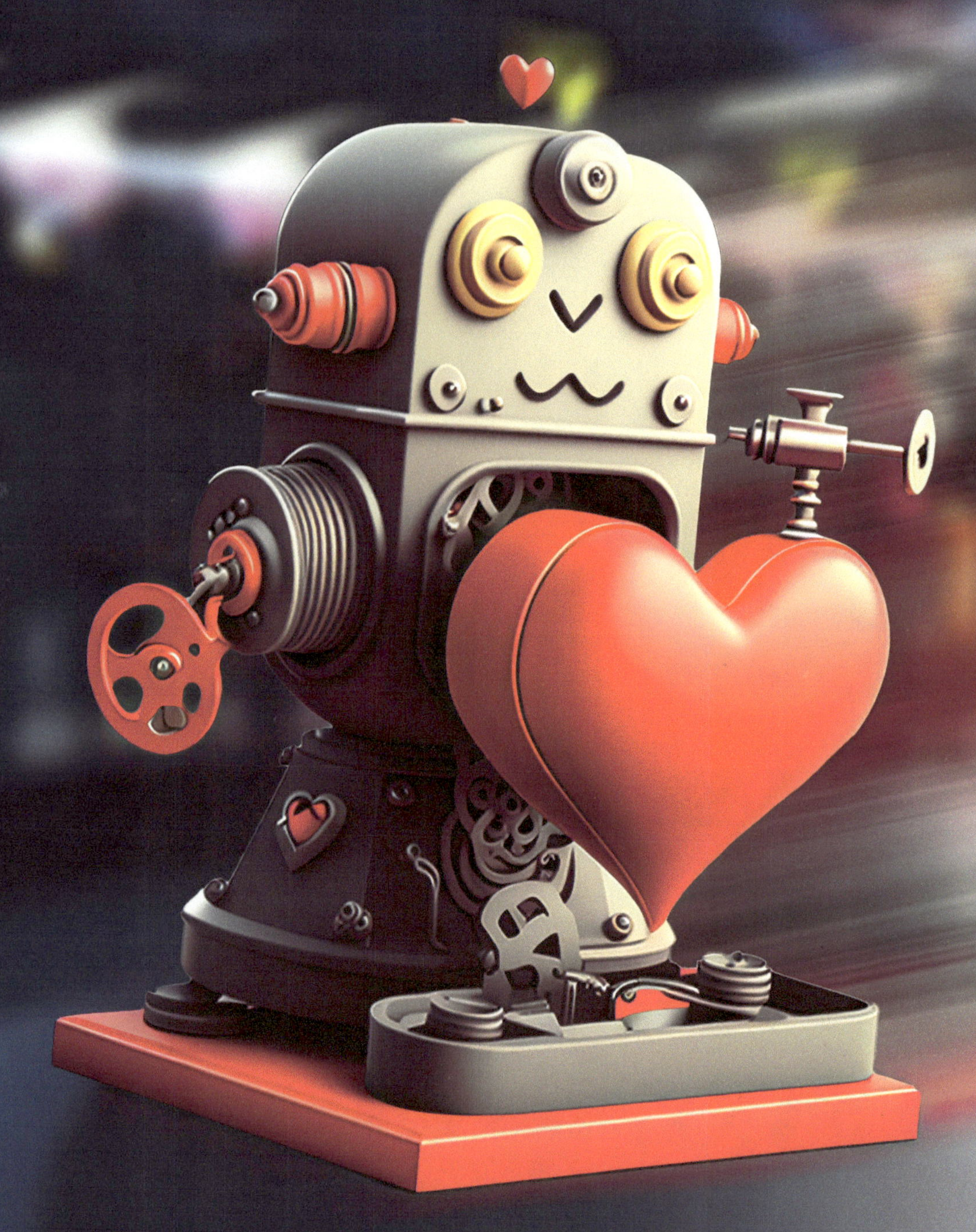

Bedazzled

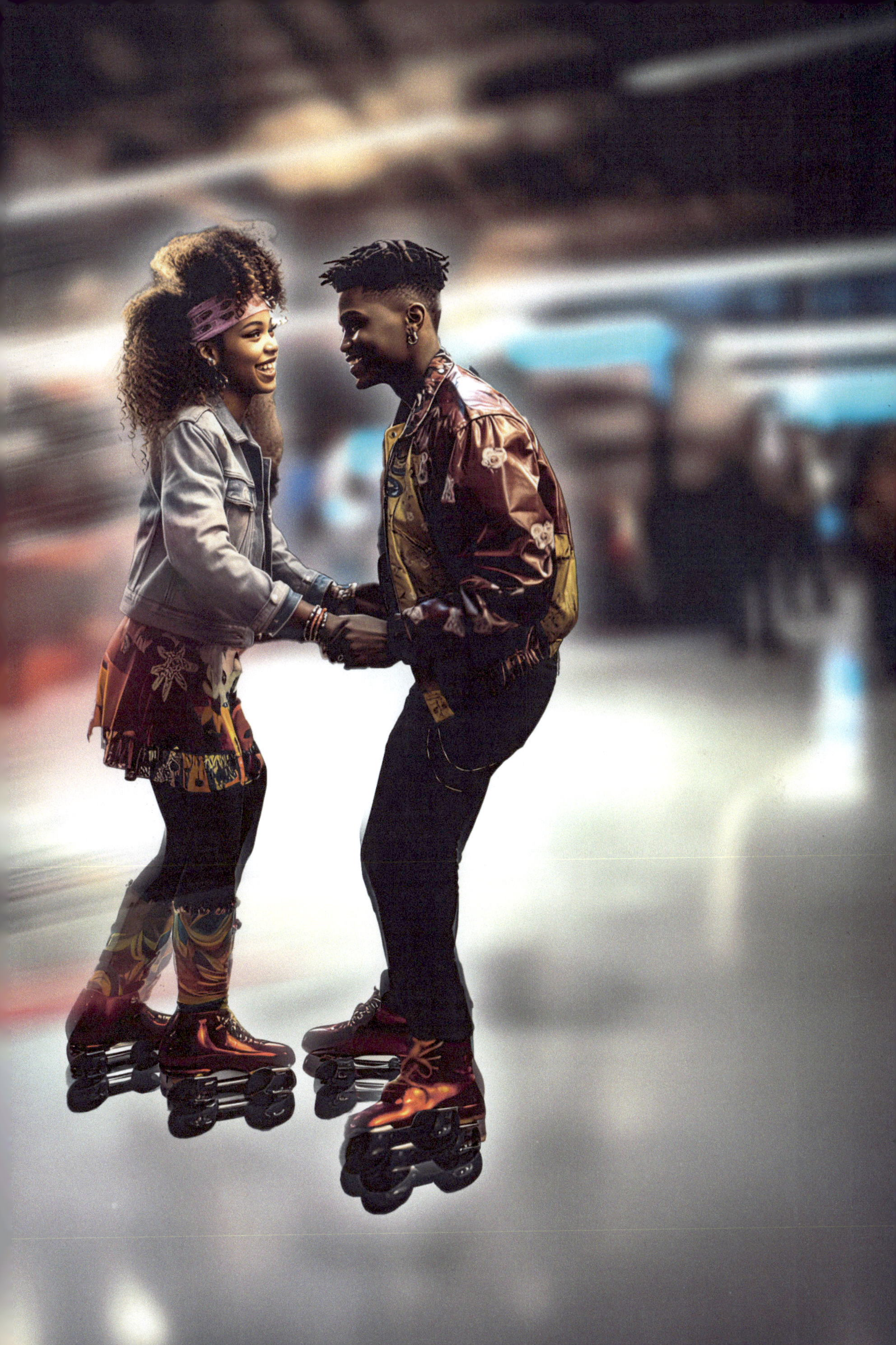

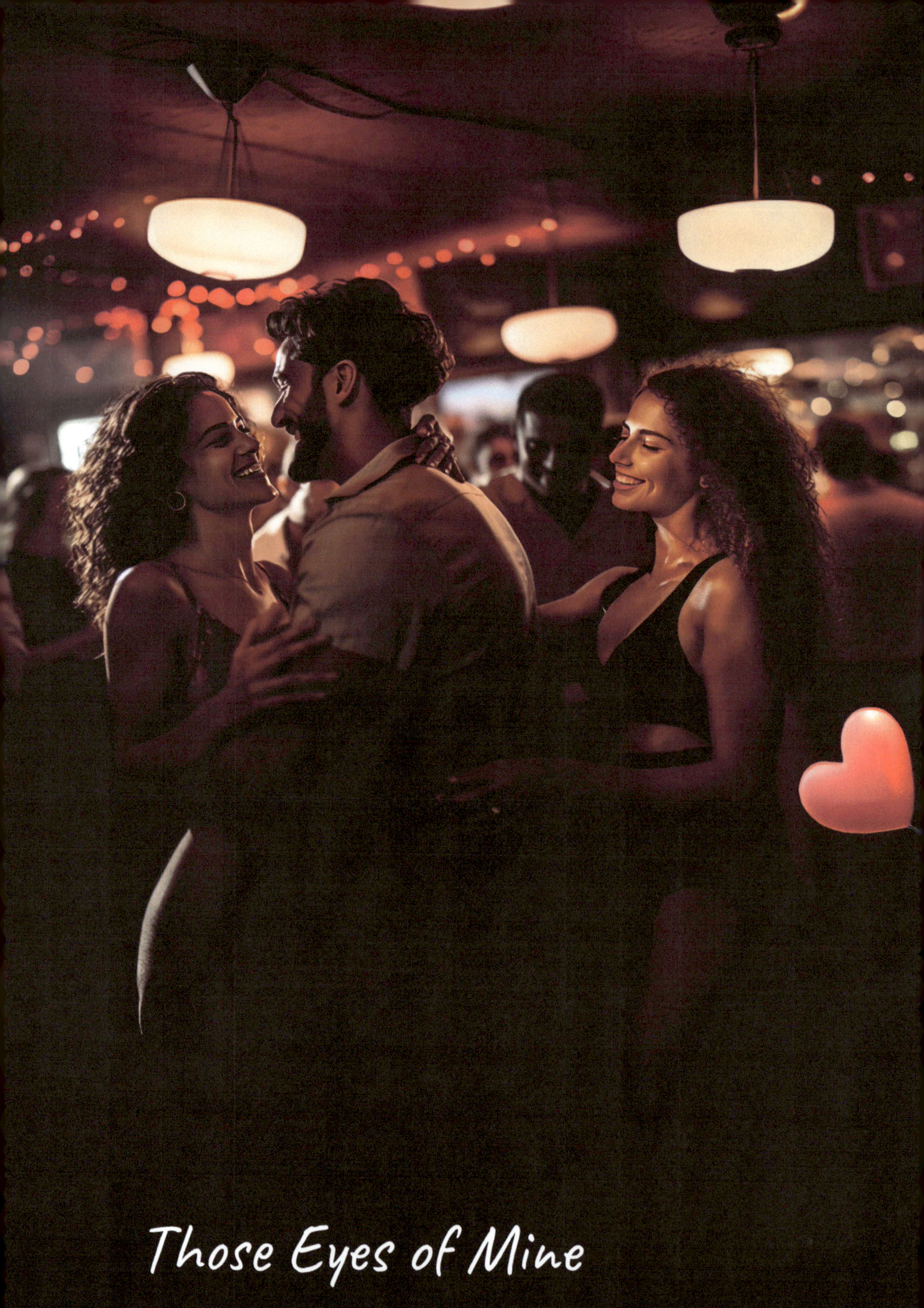
Those Eyes of Mine

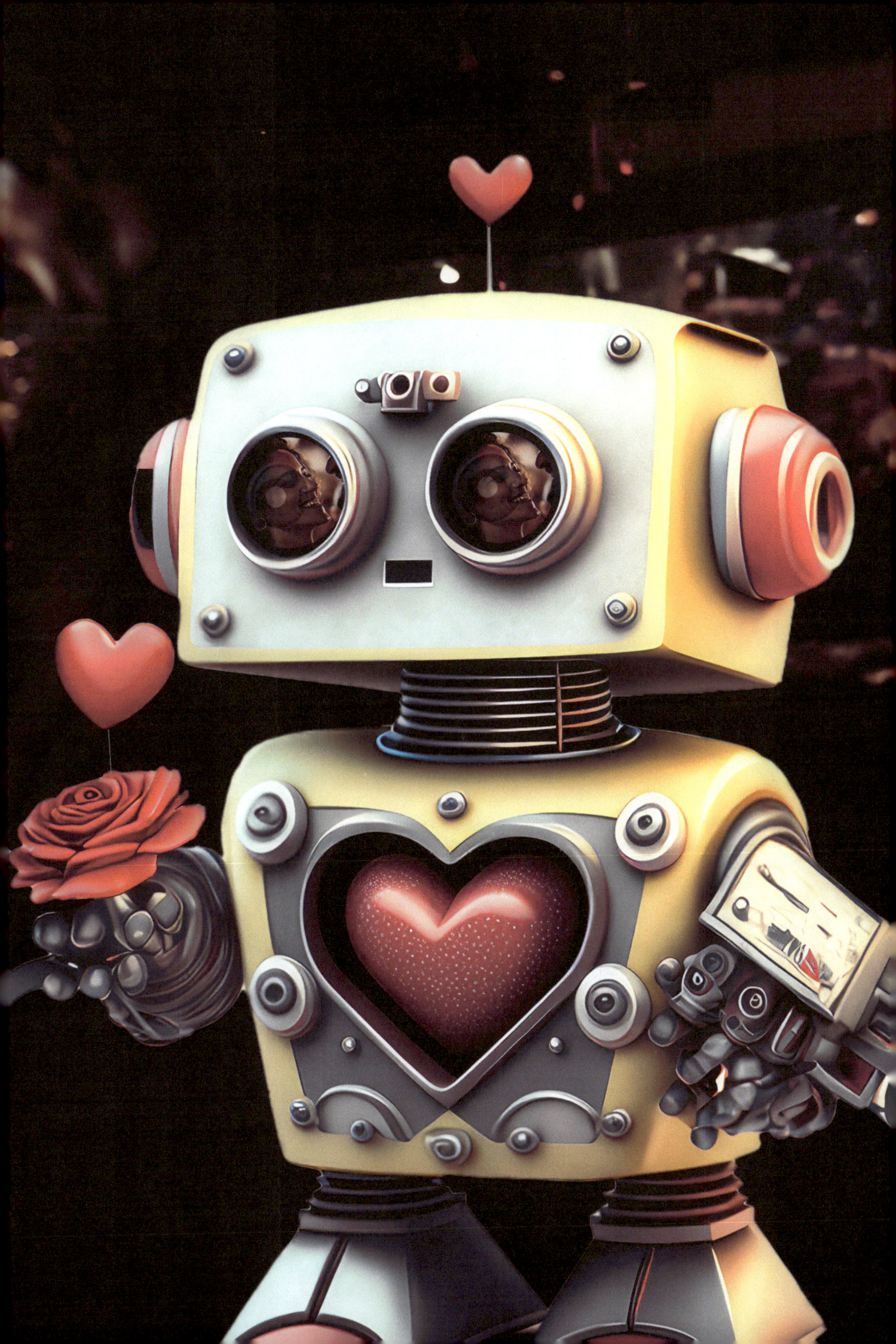

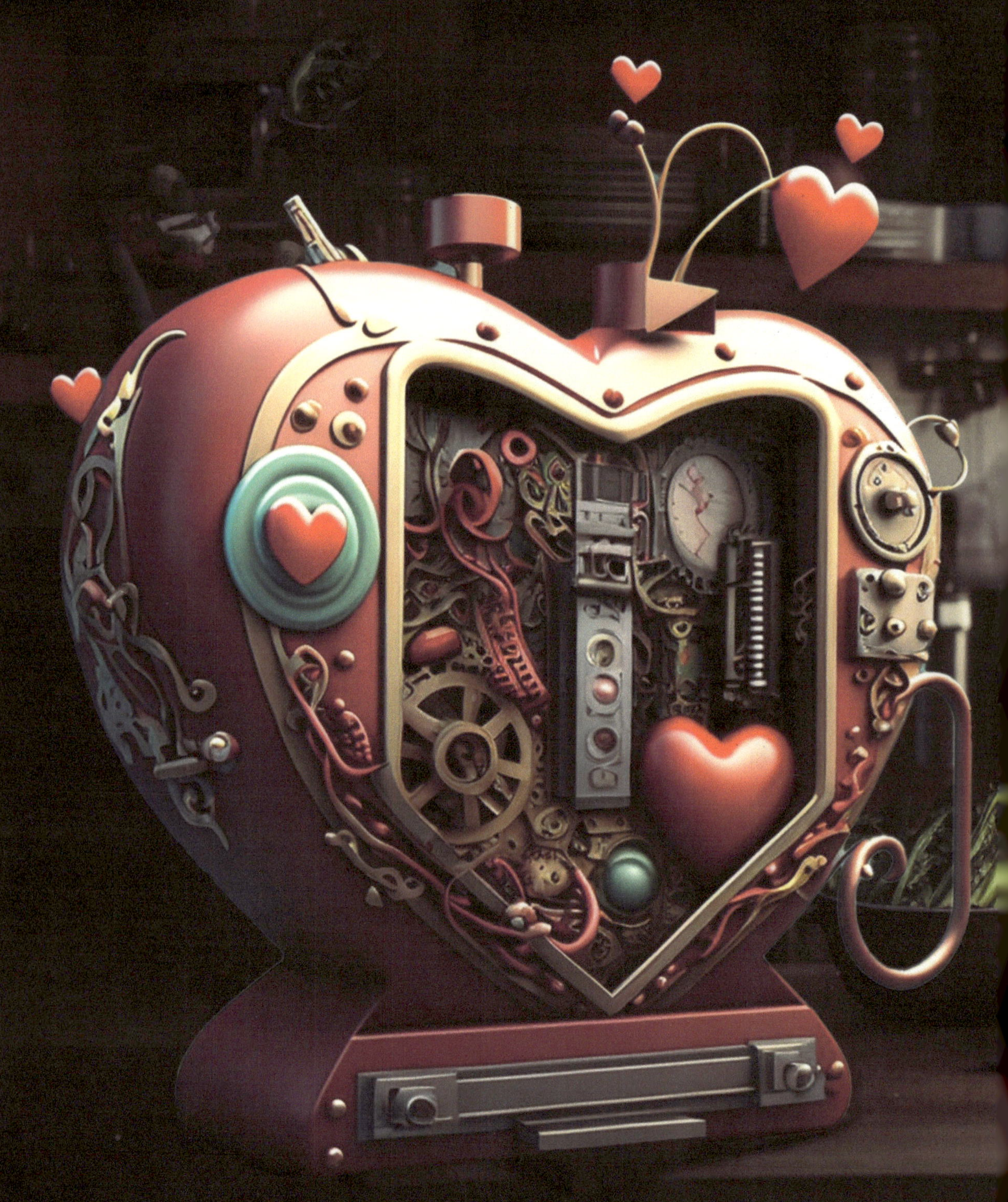

The Recipe

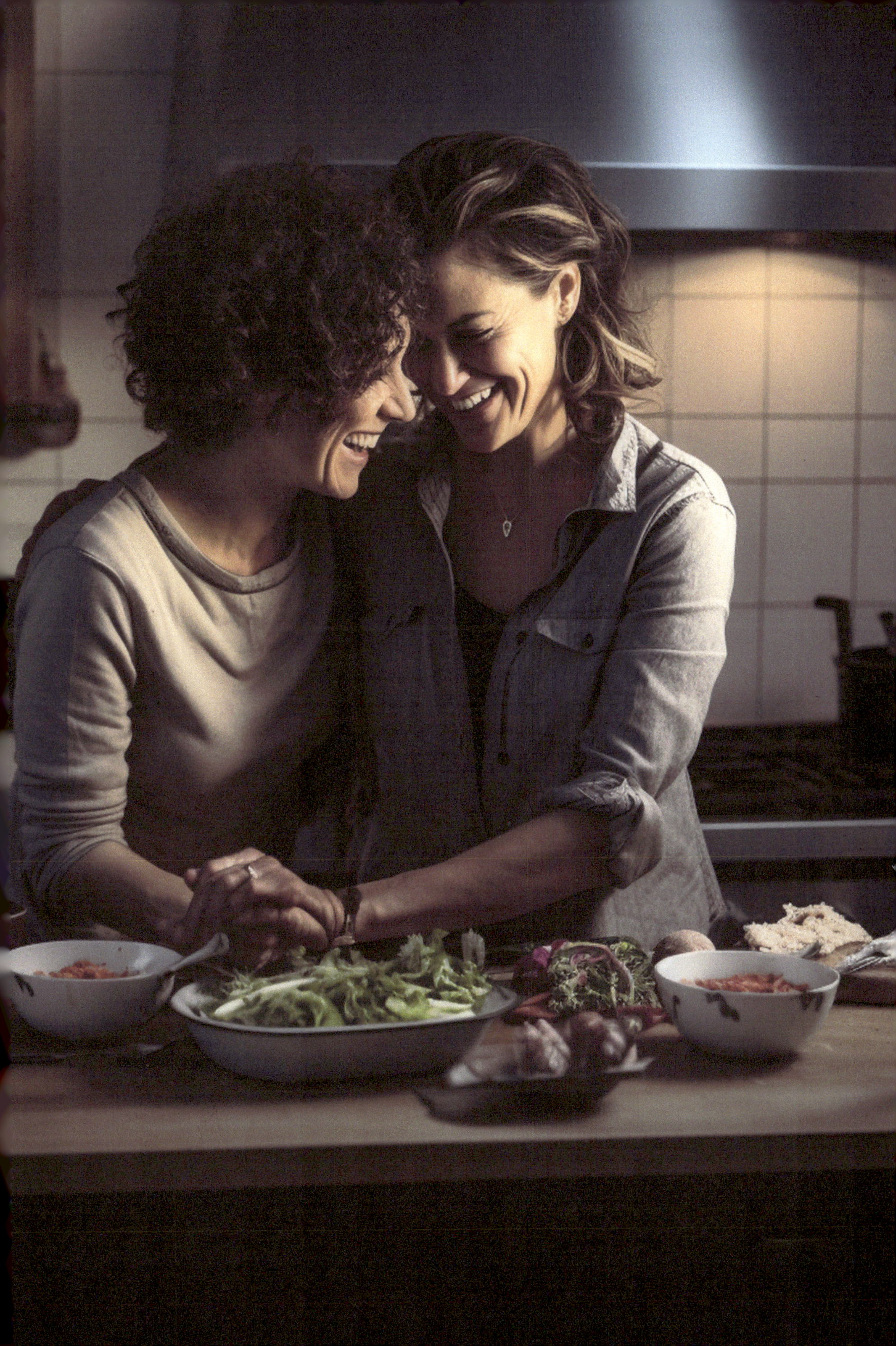

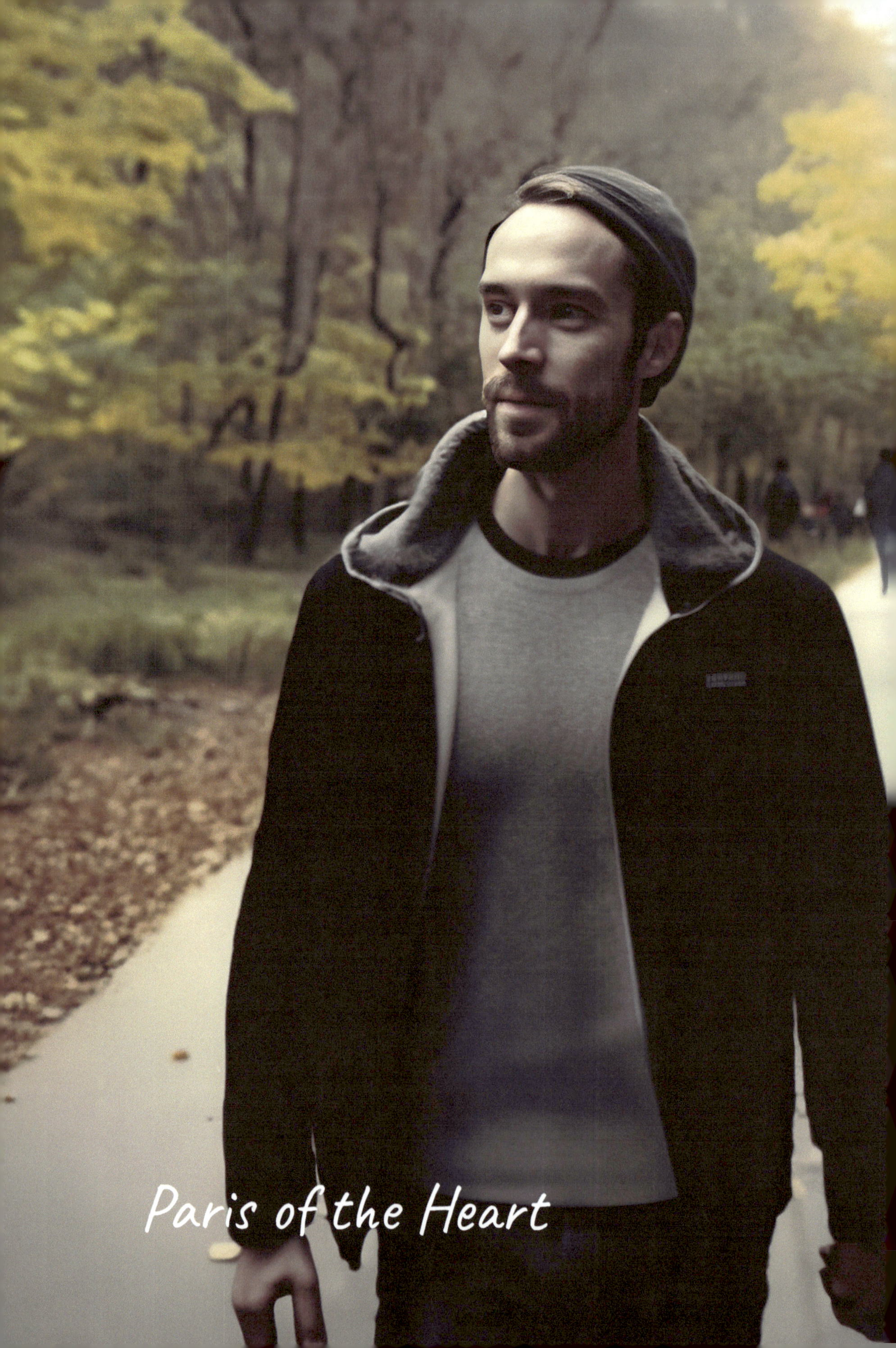
Paris of the Heart

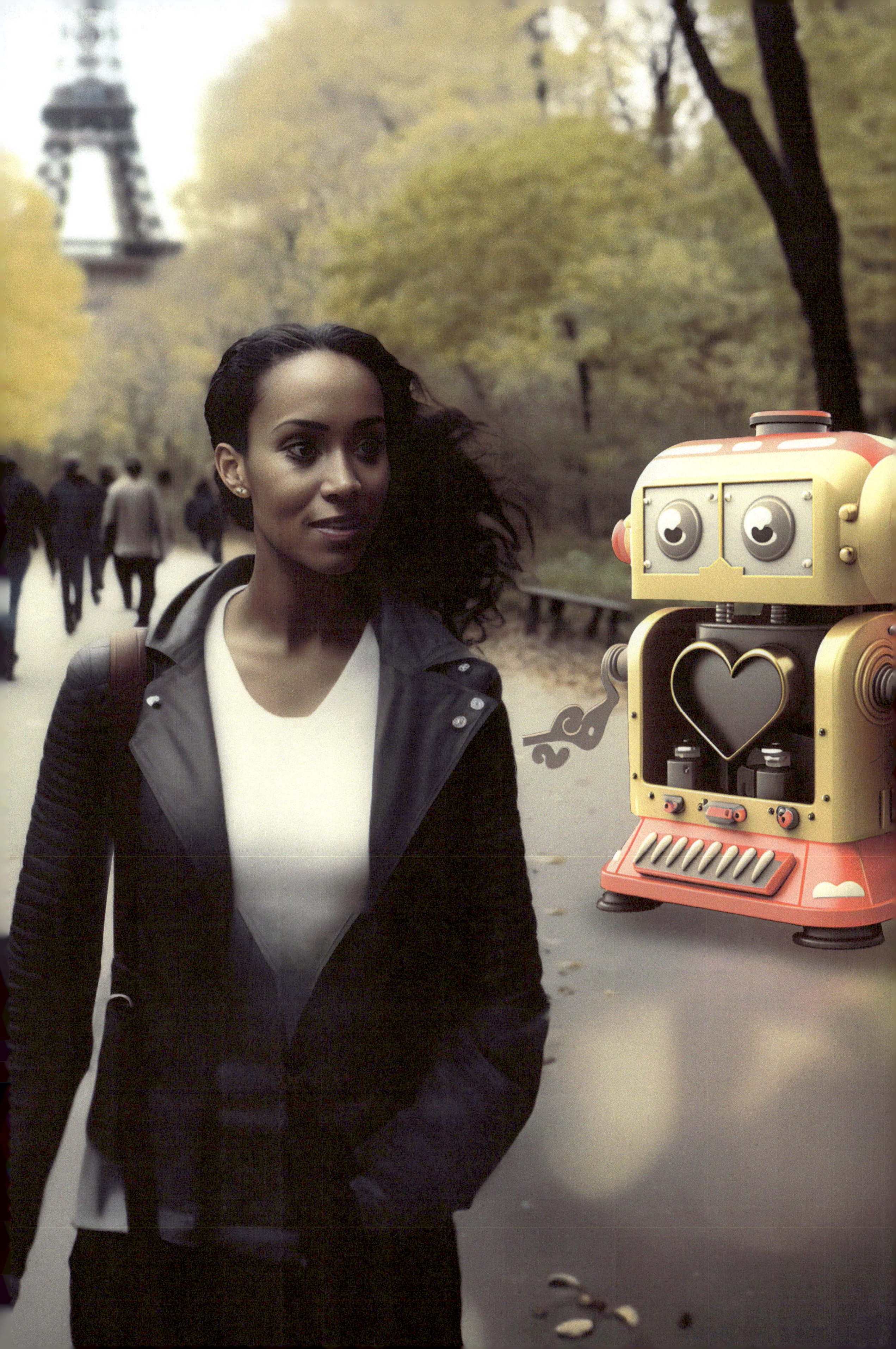

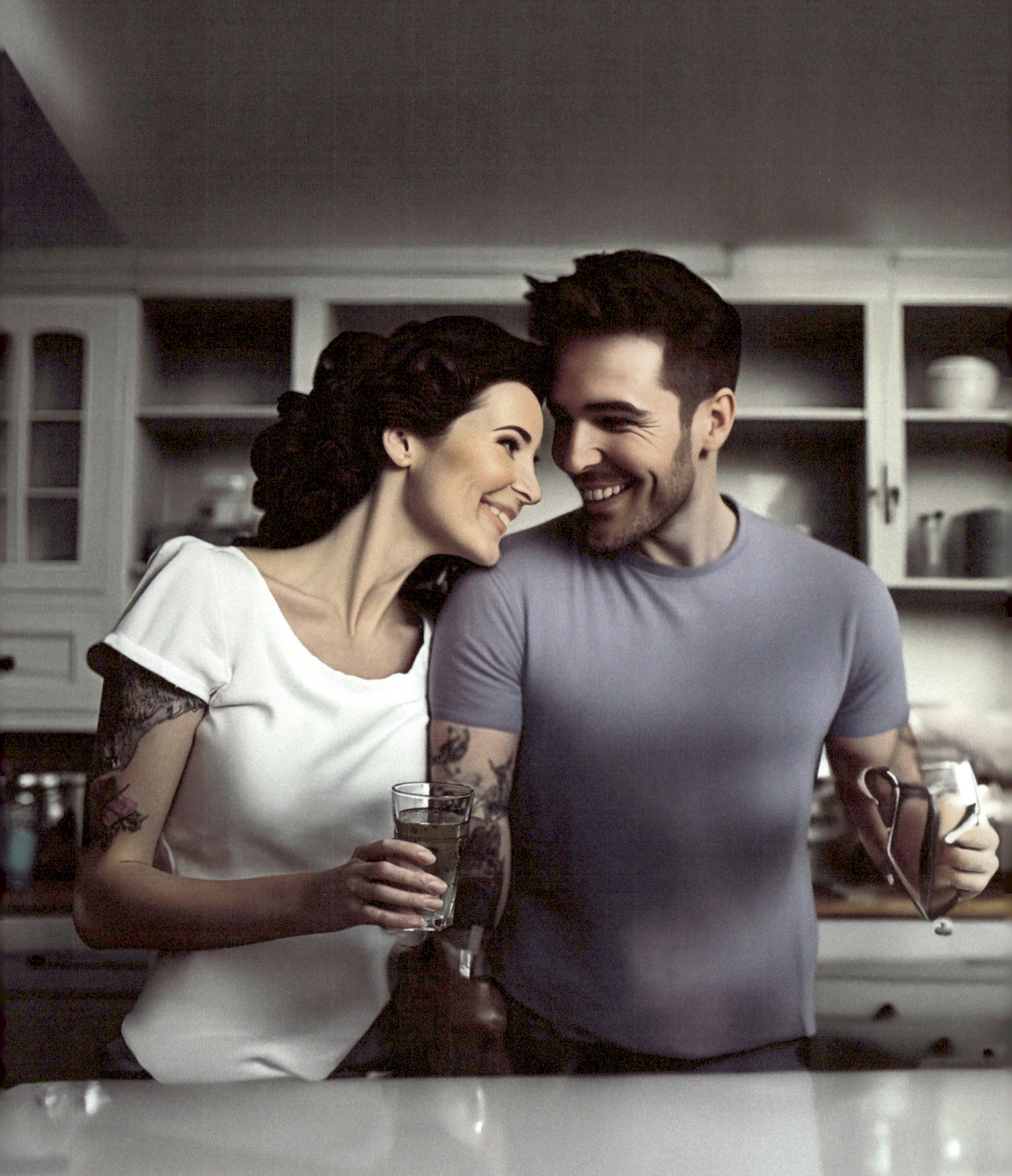

All We Need

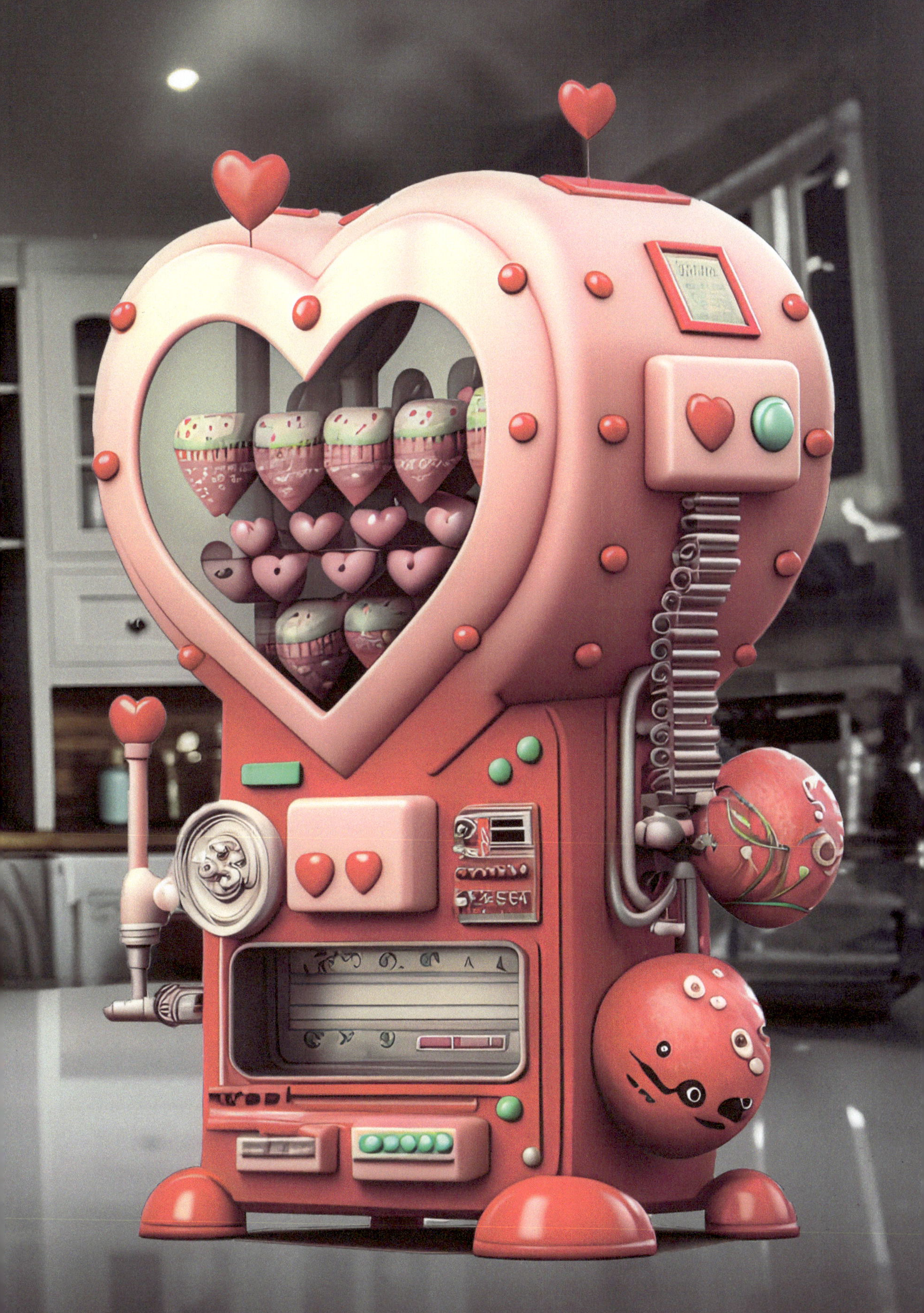

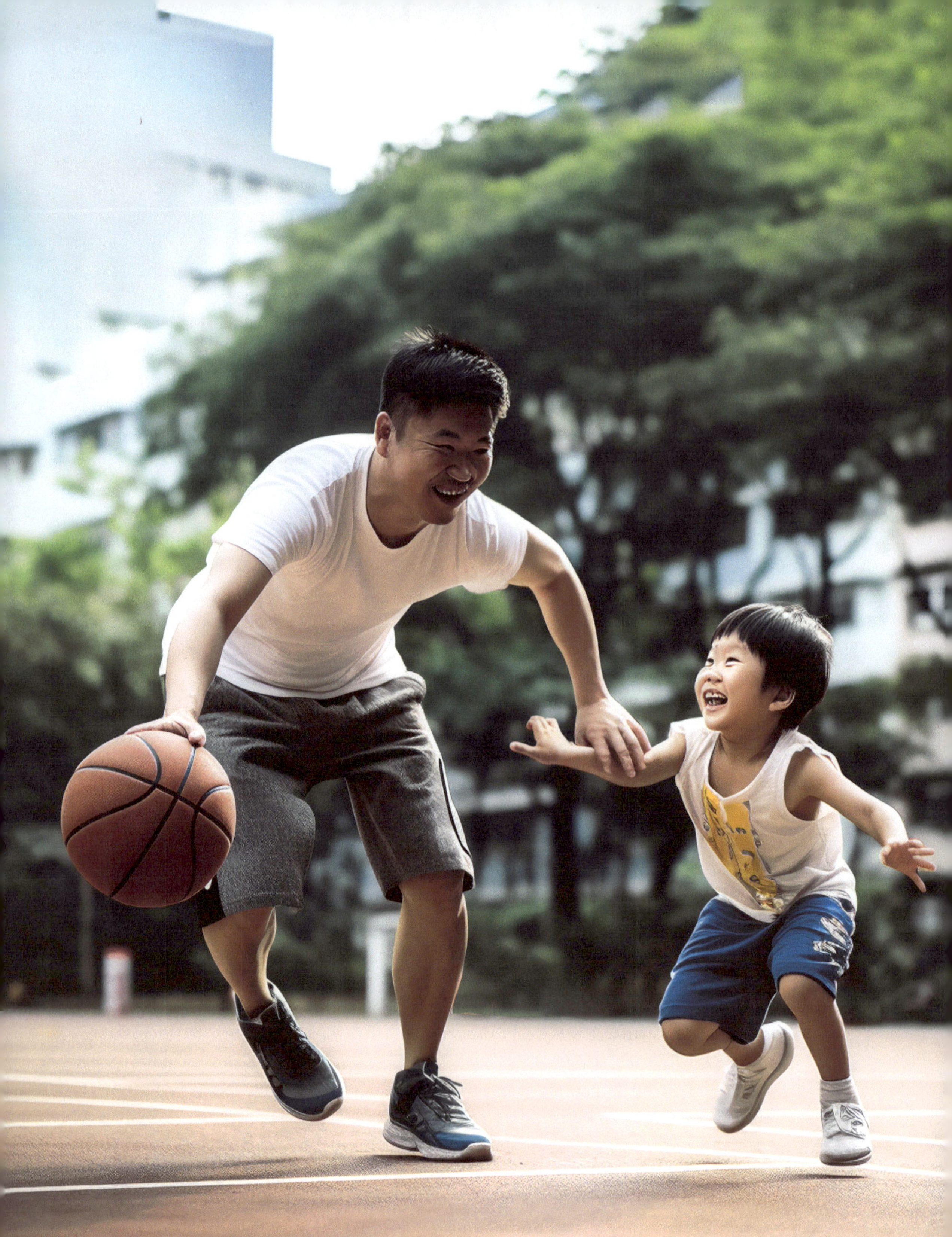

Slam Dunk Day

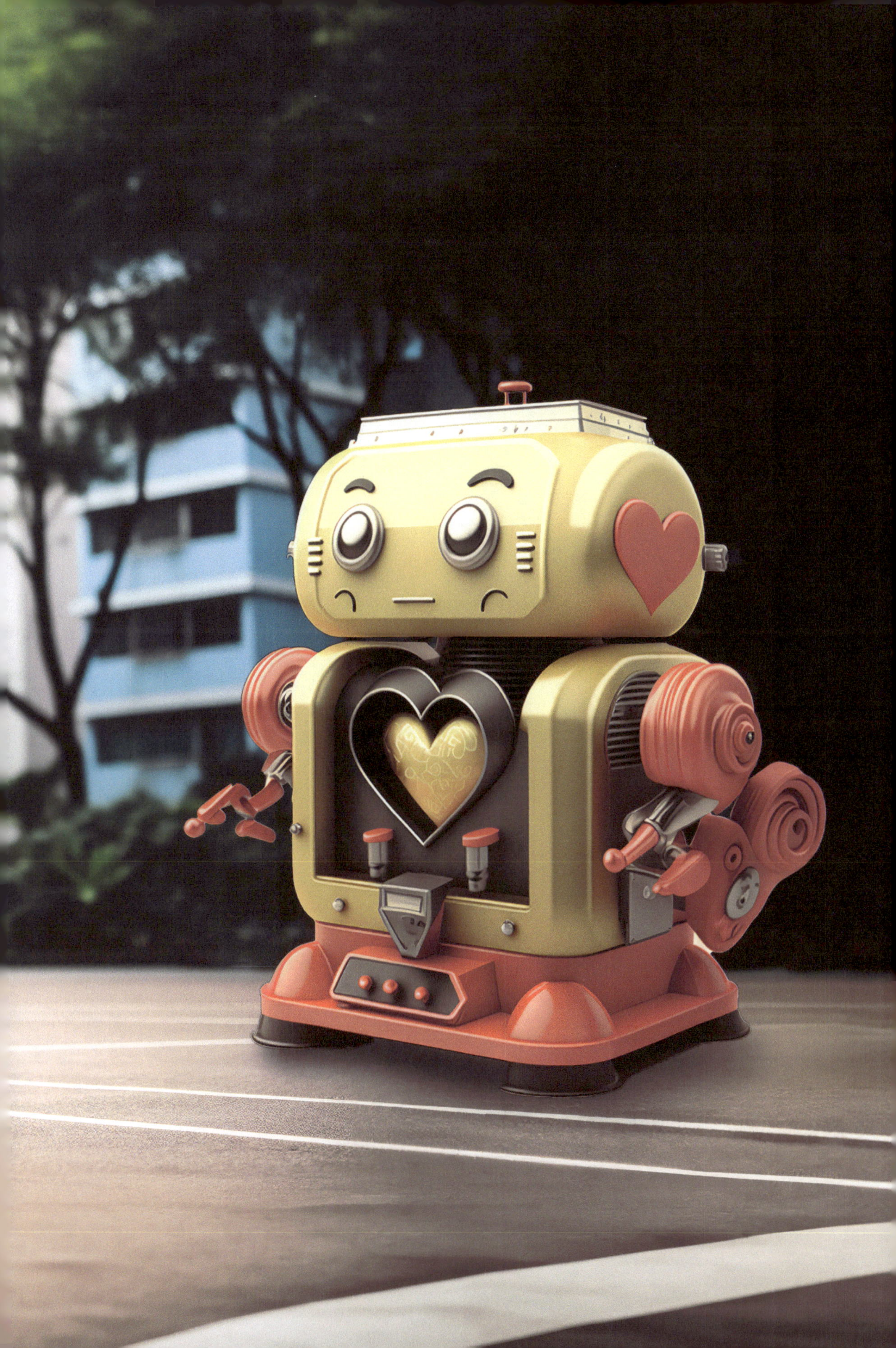

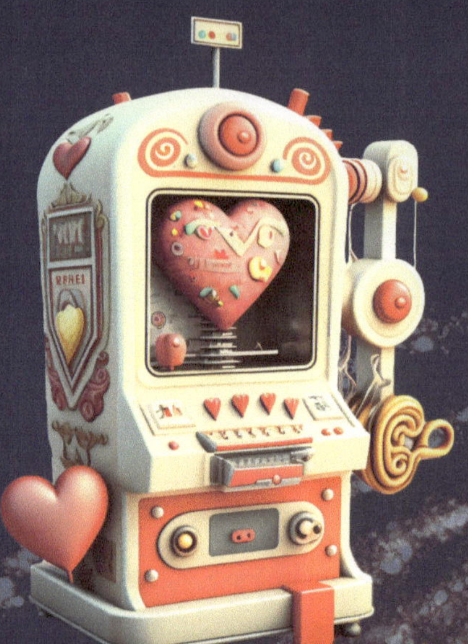

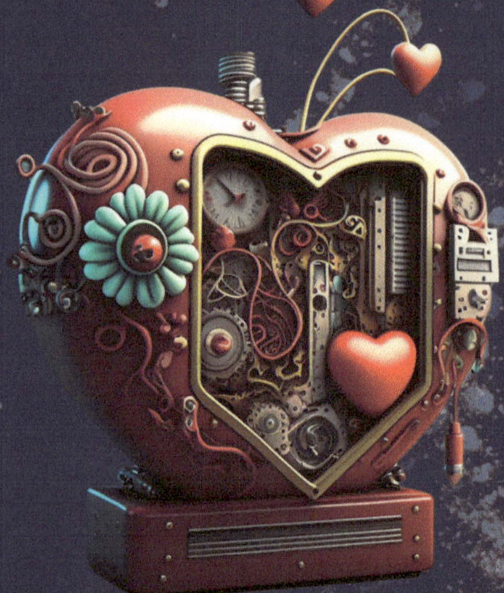

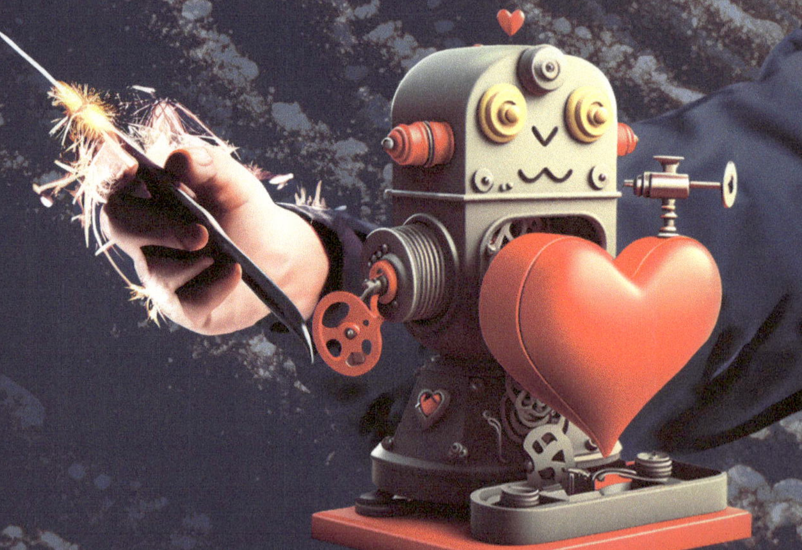

Markieji's Dream

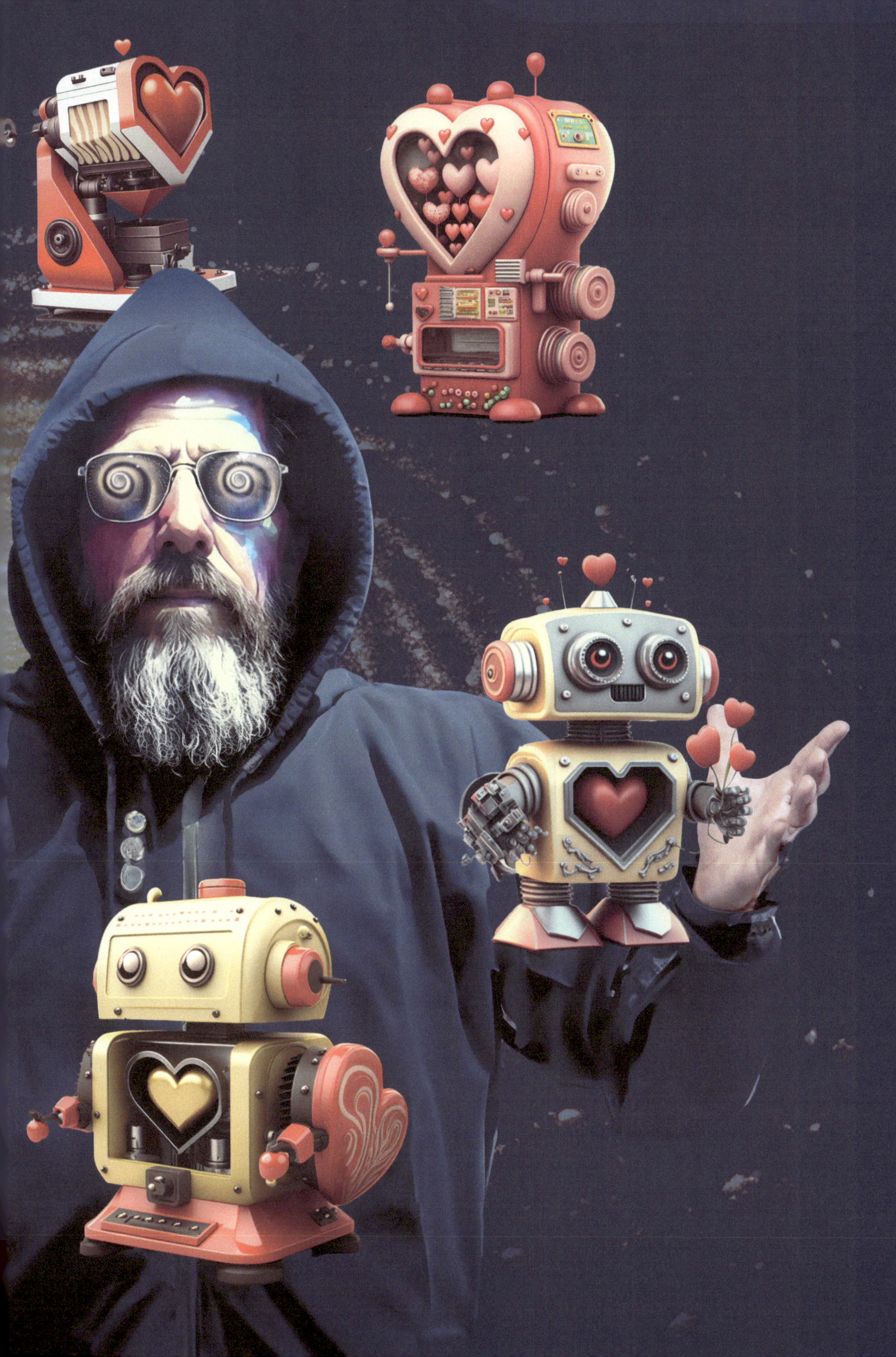

About the Author

Mark Krigbaum is an award-winning writer, producer, and director of documentaries, TV shows, and films. His work includes ***Transformation of Myth Through Time***, a PBS series with Joseph Campbell; ***The Reluctant Robot***, a children's TV science special; ***Death Makes Life Possible***, a documentary film with Deepak Chopra; and he was a producer and editor on ***Forbidden Power***, directed by legendary filmmaker Paul Kyriazi. Mark is currently in development on an animated children's music program titled ***Harmony Lane***.

Mark's pen name, Markieji, is a humorous play on his childhood nickname "Markie" combined with the suffix "ji," which is an honorific used in the Indian subcontinent. Markieji is his artist identification to distinguish from his work in media and television.

LuV MachinZ: Collection #1 is Markieji's first published book and features original art designed for NFTs, animated videos, paintings, physical art, and sculptures based on the LuV MachinZ characters.

Other NiftyArt.design projects

Ambient Glitch

ScribblZ

SMDGZZ

Pizia Tarocchi

Thank you to my wife Angela Murphy for being my editor and muse.

My gratitude to my family, my friends and Baba Hari Har Ramji whose love has inspired and informed this work

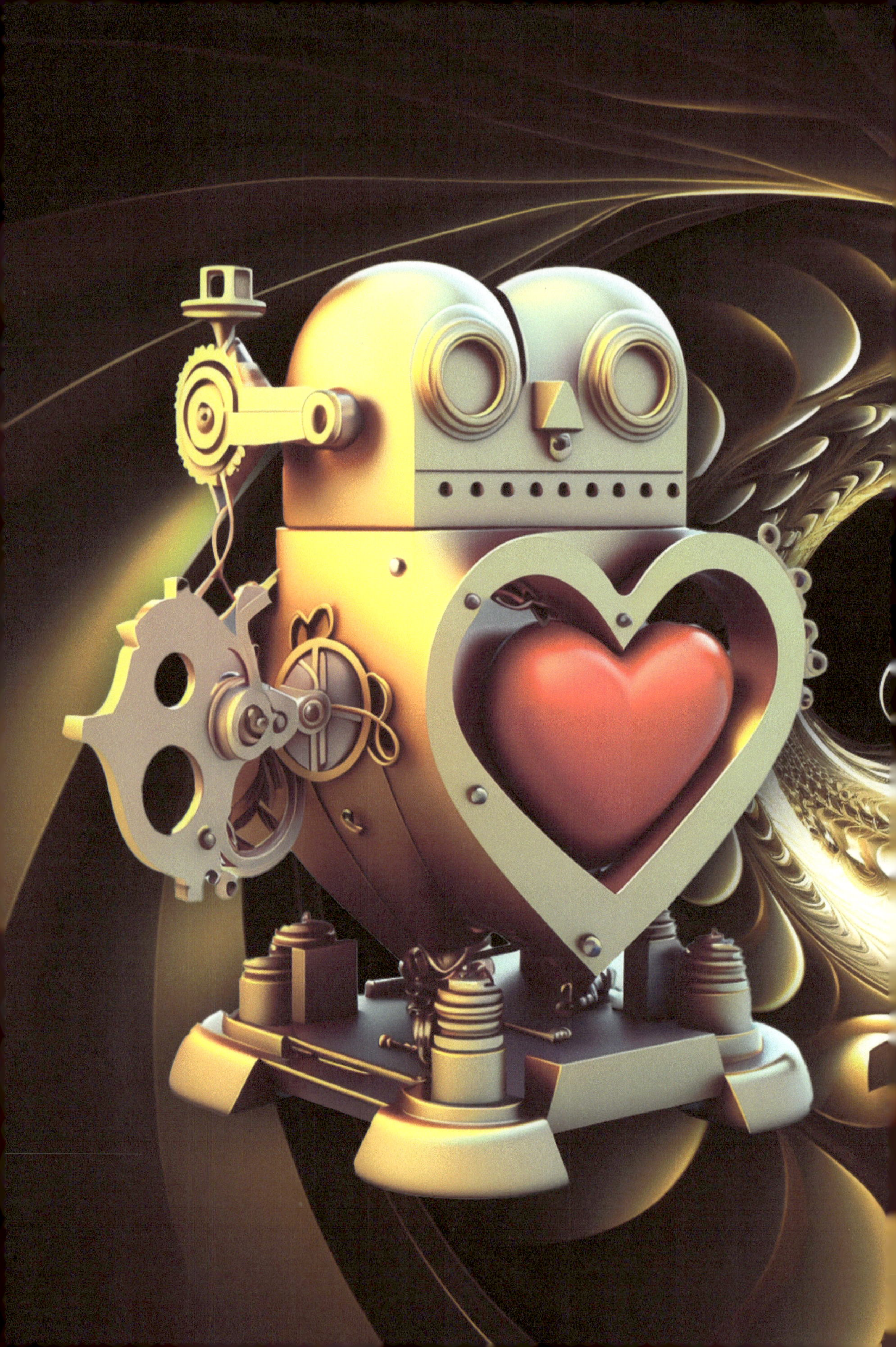

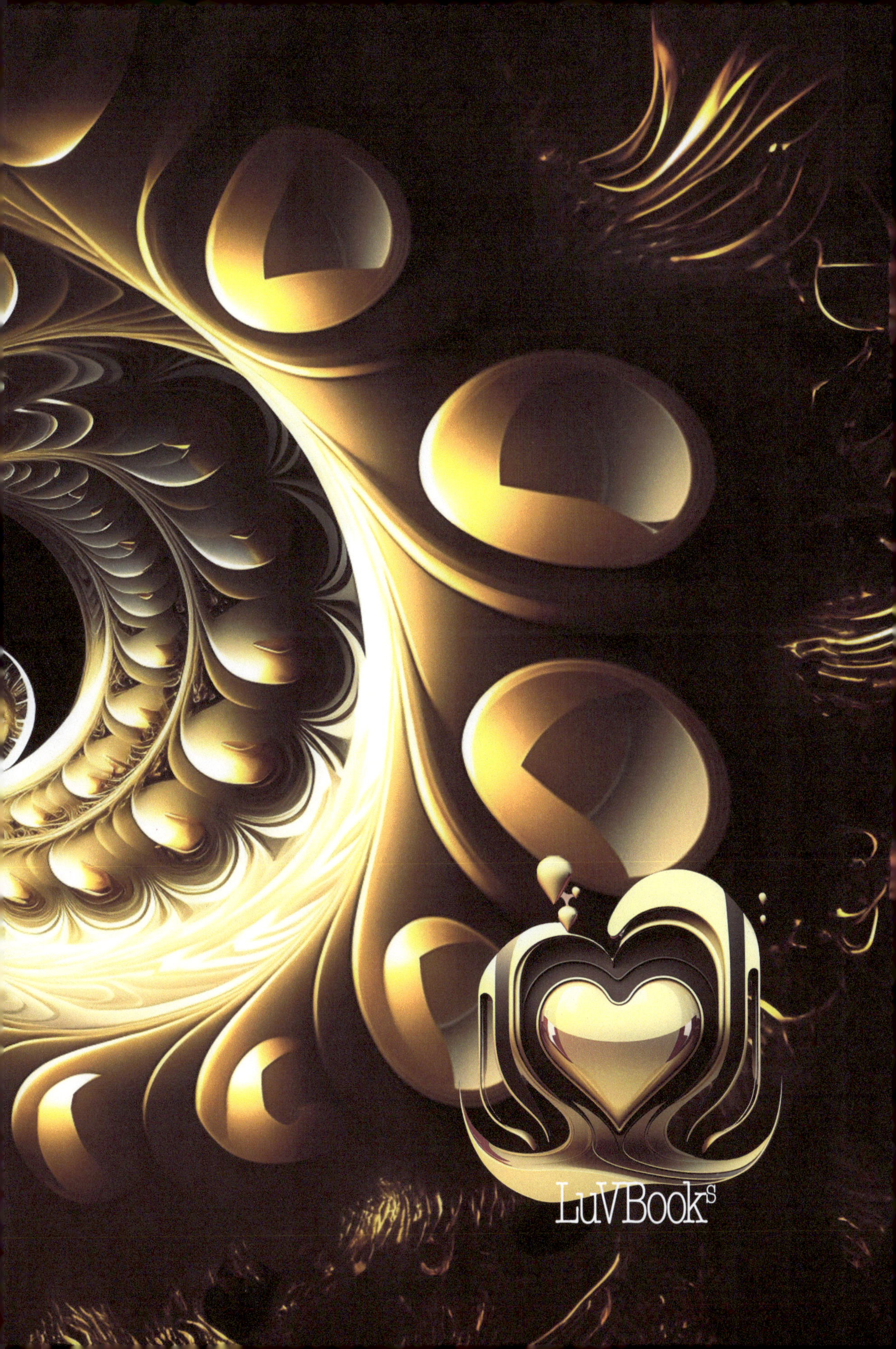
LuVBooks

www.ingramcontent.com/pod-product-compliance
Lightning Source LLC
LaVergne TN
LVHW070140110826
845147LV00002B/297

9798218321758